BEST
GAY EROTICA
OF THE YEAR

VOLUME FOUR

BEST
GAY EROTICA
OF THE YEAR

VOLUME FOUR

Edited by

ROB ROSEN

CLEiS
PRESS

Published in the United States by Cleis Press, an imprint of Start Midnight, LLC, 101 Hudson St, Suite 3705, Jersey City, NJ 07302.

Printed in the United States.
Cover design: Scott Idleman/Blink
Cover photograph: iStock
Text design: Frank Wiedemann
First Edition.
10 9 8 7 6 5 4 3 2 1

Trade paper ISBN: 978-1-62778-284-5
E-book ISBN: 978-1-62778-285-2

For my husband Kenny, my light, my love, my life

CONTENTS

INTRODUCTION

Hello, Dear Readers, and welcome to *Best Gay Erotica of the Year, Volume 4*. This is my fifth time at the helm of this esteemed collection, and I'm thrilled, as always, to be able to offer you some of the best gay literary erotica around. I had close to two hundred submissions for this issue, and to be able to whittle it down to a mere sixteen slots was next to impossible. I could've made three awesome collections from what I received, but one is all I could do, and so one super-spectacular anthology lies ahead of you—somewhat spread-eagle, in fact, and occasionally on its knees.

For those of you who are unfamiliar with my writing, I'm a romantic-comedy author by trade, frequently in the speculative genre. And so, whilst whittling—and since reading and enjoying what one is reading is oh-so subjective—I found myself choosing stories for you that fall into three categories: comedy/madcap, sci-fi/speculative, and general fiction, almost all of it of a romantic nature, a hundred percent of it of the high literary caliber that you've come to expect from this annual collection.

For comedy/madcap, there's Clare London's after-hours romp

in a dentist's office in "Open Up"; Nelson House's "Dirty Tricks," with its dirty double-crosses and sneaky Republican senator; Richard May's naughty Hanukkah-present-filled "Eight Nights"; the farcical romp through the streets of Florence, "Renaissance Miracles," by the superbly imaginative Michael Ampersant; and closing out the collection, Richard Michaels's "Forward into the Past," featuring a private dick you won't soon forget.

Sci-fi/speculative takes center stage in Jordan Castillo Price's vampiric-virus tour de force, "Appetite." Kyle E. Miller chooses humanity over the divine in "The Temptation of the Gargoyle." Vincent Meis's "Blade of Grass" takes us on an unexpected journey into Turkey. And Michael Roberts has us howling with his cloning mishap tale, "Reflections."

Interspersed throughout the collection, the literary genius continues with Landon Dixon's washed-up boxer saga, "It's Only Natural." Gregory L. Norris writes about four broke men shooting a porn movie with surprising results in "Foursome." Wayne Goodman's sensual male geisha story, "Out of Yoshiwara," has us traveling to Japan. And the ever-remarkable Dale Chase offers a glimpse into the life of a has-been actor and a winsome pool boy in "Legend."

But, of course, there're even more stories to follow, all of them expertly written and deeply erotic, all by some of today's best and brightest M/M writers, hailing from all over the United States, plus Canada, the United Kingdom, and France. So, sit back and relax—perhaps spread-eagle or on your knees, just as a suggestion—and enjoy *Best Gay Erotica of the Year, Volume 4!*

Rob Rosen
San Francisco

IT'S ONLY NATURAL

Landon Dixon

There was a knock on the door. Lloyd groaned and rolled over onto his stomach, smacking the greasy pillow with a left hook. His mouth felt like it was full of cotton, his legs heavy like after a fifteen-rounder.

The knock sounded again.

"Yeah! Come in!" Lloyd yelled into the pillow.

A bellboy in a tight, wine-colored, shiny-from-wear uniform pushed the door open with a creak and walked the heaving floorboards into the room. "Your . . ." The kid stopped, staring at Lloyd laid out on the sagging single bed.

Lloyd was naked, the dirty sheet and cover pushed down to the foot of the bed. He was clutching the pillow, lying on his stomach, his legs bent and back curved, bare buttocks mounding up high and plush.

The bellboy licked his lips and set the jug of moonshine down on a wobbly wooden table, the only stick of furniture in the dilapidated hotel room other than an equally scarred and rickety chair and the bed. "Your, uh, *hair of the dog*, Mr. Lloyd." The bellboy rubbed his damp hands on his lean thighs, still staring at Lloyd's white, naked body; at those lushly humped buttocks.

Lloyd let go of the pillow and rolled over onto his back. He smacked crusted lips and blinked bloodshot eyes, running his hands down over his broad chest. His body had slightly gone to flab, a little too soft and round in certain areas, but still fairly trim and muscular. His chest banded and stomach tightened in ribbed contours as he stretched out his well-formed arms and legs. His cock was large and languid in a nest of blond pubes, warming up like the rest of him at the sight of the jug of cheap contraband whiskey—that and the gawking young man in his room.

"What's your name, kid?" he asked, working some saliva into his mouth, then licking his red lips.

"Joey," the bellboy responded, his nervous brown eyes glued to Lloyd's cock flopped over the man's left thigh.

"You know who I am?"

"Uh, you're Mr. Lloyd. Room 313."

Lloyd let out a phlegmy chuckle. "That's who I am *now*—a bum in a crummy hotel. But I used to be Pretty Boy Lloyd, middle-weight contender."

Joey grinned. "Yeah, sure. I heard of you. My dad and I went to your fight in '49, when you KO'd Thunder Thompson in the fifth round."

Joey looked over Lloyd's body, clearly noticing the scar tissue on the man's heavy eyebrows, the cauliflowering of his left ear, the flattened bridge of Lloyd's nose, the displaced knuckles on the big, meaty hands.

"Yeah, sure. I know who you are. What happened?"

Lloyd chuckled again, deep in the barrel of his chest. He knew he could barely get by with the moniker Pretty Boy these days, too much partying when he should've been training taking as much toll on his body and his twelve-year career as the fifty-two fights he'd amassed. Now his once striking golden boy features were more spread out, softer, riper—like the tomato can at thirty he'd become. Not a contender anymore, but merely an opponent.

He looked Joey over and liked what he saw: a slender, slick-haired kid with a wet mouth and doe eyes. This was a kid who was after his own tastes, which he could tell from plenty of experience. "I'm just waiting for the right fight to come along, Joey. Training here at the hotel."

He reached down to his groin and lifted his semierect cock, then stroked it. "Want to go a few rounds with Pretty Boy, kid?" He didn't have enough money to even pay for the moonshine, let alone the room at the end of the week. He was flat broke, a beaten-down pug. But he could still get by on some of his once latent physical prowess.

Joey's lips twitched, his eyes on Lloyd's cock. The tool was swelling in the fighter's pumping hand, thick and heavy and powerful. Joey turned and locked the door, then walked toward the bed, his fingers shaking as he popped the brass buttons on his monkey suit. Lloyd's cock towered up in his swirling hand, flooding the fighter's groin and body with a warmth that smoothed the rough edges of the ugly room and the even uglier day to come.

Joey was naked by the time he reached the side of the bed where Lloyd lay on his back stroking his cock. His boyish body was pale and hairless, smooth, nipples pink and puffy, cock standing as tall and slender as he was. Lloyd reached out with his left hand and gripped Joey's cock, pulling him closer. Joey buckled and groaned, his taut buttocks clenching.

"How about giving my cock a workout, kid?" Lloyd husked, pumping the pair of pricks. "And then I'll give your cute little asshole a good hard sparring session. We'll split the jug afterward."

Joey moaned, his body bowing with the strong, gripping tug

of Lloyd's hand on his throbbing cock. Lloyd gave a hard jerk, yanking Joey right over the side of the bed and on top of him. Their cocks pressed together, pulsating against each other. Lloyd scooped up Joey's ass and kneaded the hot, humped flesh, swarming his hungry tongue all around Joey's spit-slick, open mouth. Joey grabbed on to Lloyd's close-cropped blond hair, pumping his surging cock against Lloyd's even harder prick.

They wildly kissed for a minute or so, the heat building and building, like the spunk in both sets of balls, their cocks thumping together. Then Lloyd pulled his tongue out of Joey's mouth and his hands off of Joey's rump. He gripped the young man by the bony shoulders and shoved him down to his throbbing cock, where Joey's mouth could set to work.

Joey nestled in between Lloyd's spread legs, nuzzling the man's pubic hair. Then he looked up at the twitching slab of meat and gripped it, pumping it with his hand. Lloyd bucked and grabbed on to Joey's hair. Joey shot out his pink tongue and licked up the middle of Lloyd's hairy sack, swabbing all around the man's tightened balls before grasping the cock up above.

"Yeah, that's working the bag, kid!" Lloyd grunted, riding Joey's bobbing head with his hands, his balls getting basted in a wet warmth that spread like wildfire through his tensed body in waves.

Joey licked up to Lloyd's cock, dragging his tongue all along the underside of the hard prick, leaving Lloyd's balls wet, pubes matted. He slurped the rigid pipe, painting the meat with his tongue. Lloyd arched and twisted on the creaky bed, howling when Joey finally pulled his stiff cock down and poured soft lips over the swollen tip.

"Yeah, suck it, kid!" Lloyd shouted like a trainer barking out instructions to a prospect in the gym ring. It was too much of this kind of sexercise that had set Pretty Boy's promising career on the skids. His brain had been willing, but his body had been dissipated.

Joey lifted his head higher in Lloyd's hands, sunk his mouth down lower, swallowing half of the man's wide shaft. Then he bobbed his head, pulling with his mouth, sucking Lloyd's cock quick and tight and hot and wet. Lloyd thrust his hips up, plunging his cock deeper into Joey's mouth. He pumped in rhythm, driving his cock back and forth in the young man's face.

"Fuck, kid, I'm gonna come!"

Joey sucked even harder and faster, his face burning bright, lips blossoming around the shaft, breath billowing out of his nose. He squeezed Lloyd's balls with his left hand, pumping the part of the man's shaft that wasn't in his mouth with his right, vacuuming Lloyd's cock airtight. He thumped his own leaking prick into the bed, his buttcheeks bouncing and clenching.

"Here it—"

There was a loud knock on the door.

Joey twisted his head in Lloyd's hands, his buttocks clutching. Lloyd locked Joey's head tight on his cock, the muscles popping all along his arms and on his chest. He urgently pumped into Joey's mouth.

There was another loud rap on the door. "You in there, Lloyd?! It's DeSalvo! I got a fight for ya!"

Lloyd spasmed and shouted, shooting his cock down Joey's throat. He jerked repeatedly, violently, heavy load spurting out of his face-buried prick with a blistering intensity. Joey gulped and bobbed and bounced, his own pressing cock erupting against the sheet, spouting out his own dirty joy.

"You hear me, Lloyd?! I got a fucking fight for ya!"

"Yeah! Yeah!" Pretty Boy gasped, bucking and blasting out the last of his lust into Joey's mouth. He flopped back on the bed, utterly exhausted and bent way out of shape.

* * *

His opponent was Amos Washington, aka *The Natural*, a tall, powerfully built young man with a smooth style and a thunderous, crowd-pleasing left hook. He was shy and polite, with dark good looks and an articulate way of speaking, that and a fearsome work ethic. He was an up-and-comer with a perfect 15-0 record and a telegenic personality perfectly suited for the *Friday Night Fights* that were now being broadcast by the network into American homes. Pretty Boy Lloyd was a pale, pudgy contrast, an over-the-hill fighter with a decent record and little chance of improving it, an opponent that would look good on The Natural's record.

The press conference where they signed the contract was brief but well attended. Lloyd wasn't asked a single question. As he shook hands with the clean-cut, smiling Washington, he tried to rattle the young fighter, gripping the man's hand hard and jerking on it, sticking his pug-shaped, pretty face into Washington's. But it was Lloyd who was rattled, especially when Washington's winning white smile blazed wider and his dark hand gripped harder, shoving Lloyd back with a strength that surprised the older fighter.

"This is it," DeSalvo told Lloyd later at the gym. "You gotta train serious for this one, Pretty Boy. There's big TV money at stake now. The ratings were gangbusters in '57 and they're still gettin' better. You can maybe sock away a nice retirement egg with a few good fights. Whatya say?"

Lloyd nodded his blond head, sticking his swollen hands into the sixteen-ounce training gloves as he chewed on his rubber mouthpiece, mulling over his strategy for the fight. He *was* going to train hard this time; he badly needed the money. But he also knew he needed more than mere training—he needed an edge. The Natural was simply too young and strong and quick, had too many tools that made up for his lack of experience.

DeSalvo scrambled out of the ring as Lloyd spun around,

taking a left hook square to his headgear from the young black fighter they'd brought in as a sparring partner. Lloyd staggered back against the ropes, dazed. Yeah, he was going to need an edge, all right.

The Natural's camp was ten miles outside of the city, on a farm. He was putting in the long, hard hours of training: roadwork and sparring and skipping rope, push-ups and sit-ups, throwing in some clean-living wood-chopping and brush-clearing to go along with the regular rigorous workout routines. Lloyd showed up at the camp just after nine at night, parking out on the highway before traipsing through the trees that formed a windbreak on one side of the white clapboard house and barn.

Washington was still in the makeshift ring in back of the barn, doing some shadow-boxing in the deepening evening shadows. Lloyd watched the young fighter from behind a tree trunk. It was a warm spring night. Washington was only wearing a pair of white shorts, his muscles gleaming in the moonlight as he jabbed and danced and hooked and crossed.

Lloyd gripped the bark of the tree, mesmerized. The Natural *was* a natural. He moved with a powerful fluidity that would put the Pretty Boy to shame. Lloyd's reflexes were still pretty good and he still packed a wallop, but not to this kid's extent.

He moved out from behind the tree and walked up to the ring. He had to do *something* to disrupt Washington. Only, he didn't know what—at least not yet.

"Working hard, huh?" he said in greeting.

Washington stopped popping the left and looked down at Lloyd. "Hey, Mr. Lloyd! What are you doing all the way out here?"

Lloyd grabbed on to a rope and swung up onto the ring apron, slipping through the ropes and into the ring with his opponent. "Just thought I'd get some fresh air."

The Natural looked huge in the small, tight, white shorts, his legs long and lithe, thighs corded with muscle, torso flaring up out of the trunks into a broad chest humped with more muscles, his arms long and powerful looking. Lloyd felt his legs weaken—and not just with well-merited fear.

"Mind if I do a little shadow-boxing myself?"

Washington grinned and pointed a gloved hand at the discarded set of boxing gloves lying in a corner of the ring. Lloyd smiled back, then stripped off his shirt and picked up the muffs and popped his mitts into them, then started jabbing the air like Washington.

They spun and weaved around the ring, shooting out combinations, grunting and snorting. Inevitably, they drew closer and closer to each other inside the ring. Washington's speed was astonishing, his gloves slicing dangerously through the air. Lloyd bumped into him, good-naturedly pushing him up against the ropes before landing a soft, quick combo to The Natural's shoulders.

His gloves bounced off the hard muscles. Washington good-naturedly cuffed him on the side of the head with a punch Lloyd never saw coming. Pretty Boy staggered to the side, The Natural's god-given strength shocking him all over again.

He backed off, feinted a left to the midriff, brought the left up in a jab to the face, testing Washington's commitment to his handsome exterior. Some fighters were just plain afraid of getting their features rearranged, would do anything to avoid a punch to the face. Pretty Boy knew all about that himself.

But The Natural just rolled his head to the side and grinned, cuffing Lloyd with a left hook that sent the seasoned veteran stumbling the other way. Lloyd quickly regrouped, jabbed at Washington's face, and then banged a right hand in underneath, against Washington's kidney. Some body-beautifuls couldn't take it to the torso, to the kidneys, ribs, and stomach. Washington, though, merely took a step back and then shot out a right that slammed into Lloyd's short ribs and gushed breath out of his mouth.

Lloyd fell up against Washington, grabbed on, gasping for air. In his groping mind, he realized that the only thing that was going to stop The Natural from taking him apart in the ring was a gun with a full load in every chamber. He clung to the slick, muscled fighter, reeling—in more ways than one.

But as he pressed his bare chest into Washington's bare chest, held his arms tight around the man's torso, he suddenly felt something weaken inside his opponent. It was like the other fighter had gone soft with their hot, damp skin kissing together, their chests heaving against each other, their nipples rubbing.

Lloyd thrilled with excitement and energy.

He lifted his head off Washington's chiseled shoulder and looked him dead in the eyes. The young man's dark peepers were hooded, his thick lips parted, face slack. Lloyd clenched him tighter, squishing their hard nipples together. He thrust his lower body in closer, their cocks rubbing—heavy and heated and swelling, in fact. Washington softly moaned in Lloyd's face, eyelids fluttering.

Lloyd exulted, rubbing his chest into Washington's chest, his cock into Washington's cock, the pair moving across the moonlit ring in a sensuous, sweaty slow-dance. Pretty Boy had found The Natural's weakness—and he shared it. The clean-cut All-American, it seemed, was infatuated with men. And so Lloyd bobbed his head closer and kissed Washington square on the lips.

The young man seemed to melt in his arms, his cock jumping against Lloyd's pressing prick. Lloyd kissed him again, letting it linger this time, soft and wet and sensual, their cocks still pressed up snug, nipples still melded together.

The Natural went true to his nature, almost swooning in Pretty Boy's arms, awkwardly kissing Lloyd back. Then Lloyd felt Washington's cock spasm, the man jerking in his arms as a groan escaped from between his full pink lips. He felt the sudden wetness against his crotch—the spreading come-stain from Washington's spurting prick.

Lloyd sealed his lips to Washington's gasping mouth and held the man tight in the clench, rocking with the shuddering joy. It looked like the wily veteran could teach the young, inexperienced pugilist something after all—at least in the sexual arena.

"Now, ya know I don't like ta pry," DeSalvo said the next day at the gym.

Lloyd grinned and nodded, pounding on the heavy bag. Like hell the greasy guy didn't like to pry; like every good trainer, he was part mother hen.

"But I want ya to cut out all the *bedwork*, if ya know what I mean. Sex kills the legs. So, for once in your boxing life, Lloyd, I'm beggin' ya, knock it off with the dames, okay? After all, we got three weeks to go to the match." DeSalvo's liquid-brown eyes went puppy-dog pleading. "Don't leave your game in the hotel room this time, huh, Pretty Boy. Let's just concentrate on the fight."

Lloyd hammered a right into the big bag DeSalvo was clutching, knocking his trainer backward. He followed it up with a lightning-quick, thunder-heavy series of lefts and rights. "Okay, you got it, boss," he told the rattled old man.

And this time, for once in his fight life, Pretty Boy actually meant it.

But that didn't stop Lloyd from meeting up with Washington in his crummy hotel room after both men had put in their training for the day. The Natural shut the warped door and darted his eyes around the threadbare room. "I—I really shouldn't be here," he stammered, his voice breaking. "My trainer thinks I'm sleeping in my bunk back on the farm."

Lloyd took the young man's trembling hand and placed it on his crotch, planting his own hand on Washington's. The Natural's fine features went fluid, his eyes glazing over and his mouth dropping open. He really *was* green when it came to guy-love. Still, he seemed eager to learn.

Lloyd didn't waste any time. He kissed Washington, ran his tongue around the man's full lips. Then he pulled back, yanking Washington's T-shirt out of his pants and up over his head. The fighter's bare chest gleamed darkly in the dim light. Lloyd lowered his head and touched his pink tongue to one equally pink nipple, then the other. Washington gasped and shivered.

Lloyd placed his hands on the man's chest and dug his fingers in, kneading the fibrous muscles. He took a hard nipple into his mouth and sucked on it, then bounced his head over and sucked on the twin. Washington gulped and shuddered. Lloyd could feel the throbbing need of the man through the thick nipple in his mouth. He dragged his tongue down Washington's ridged stomach to the guy's belt buckle as he sank down to his knees.

Looking up at the gaping man, Lloyd unfastened the belt, unbuttoned the pants, stuck his hand inside and pulled out the long, hard, pulsating pole that truly and fully revealed Washington's passion for his fellow man. Lloyd wrapped his pale, skilled fingers around the wrist-thick shaft and shunted his warm palm up and down the forearm-long length of Washington's unabashed manhood.

"Oh yes. Please," The Natural groaned, a tear of precome sprouting up and glistening in the yawning slit.

Lloyd lapped up the salty drop of spunk, pumping his hand up and down the pulsing snake. He barely had time to suck the domed hood into his mouth, tug on it with his lips, before Washington grabbed on to his head and groaned in sexual agony, shooting his heavy load into Lloyd's mouth.

Washington jerked around like a puppet on a string, Lloyd playing the young man's spouting pipe with his pumping hand and sucking mouth. He swallowed just as fast as Washington spurted, drinking in The Natural's strength straight from the hose.

They weren't done for that night, though, not by a long shot. Washington had a capacity for recovery—and sperm. Lloyd led him over to the bed. He stripped off his clothes, crawling onto the bed on all fours.

"I—I can put my . . . my pecker in your ass?" Washington asked, fresh-faced and hard-hung.

"You'd better," Lloyd responded, grinning.

But when the young man jumped onto the bed behind the older man and tried to plow his reconstituted dong into Lloyd's dry asshole, the veteran had to show him the ropes about lube.

Once properly greased, Lloyd pressed his face into the sheets and reached back with one hand to spread his plump cheeks, then reached back with his other hand and planted Washington's mushroomed hood into his parted pink pucker. Washington moaned when cock-skin met ass-skin, then howled when Lloyd pushed his ass back, plunging a third of Washington's dong through his ring and into his chute. The Natural excitedly drove the rest home, slamming his prick into Pretty Boy's tight hole.

"Oh god! Yes! Yes!" Washington cried out, his entire cock squeezed hot and tight in Lloyd's ass.

Lloyd had to push back even more, bounce his buttcheeks off Washington's trembling thighs, to get the man fucking, to experience the true pleasure of penetrating another man's ass. Washington gripped Lloyd's waist and exuberantly pounded into Lloyd's hole, his huge, churning cock searing Lloyd's man-tunnel.

It took a ton of willpower that Pretty Boy didn't even know he possessed to stop himself from grabbing on to his own flopping hard cock to jack out his own steaming joy, but he resisted the urge, rocking back and forth to The Natural's raucous banging. The young man shouted, jerked, spasmed off Lloyd's rippling cheeks. It was then that Lloyd felt another huge, hot load spout inside of him, tasting it with his bowels this time.

Washington came with a thunderous disregard for the consequences, letting loose for possibly the first time in his life. He poured his essence into Lloyd's chute and then collapsed on top of his opponent, spent and exulted. This was surely a hundred times more satisfying than knocking out another fighter in the ring.

Pretty Boy kept after his man. The Natural needed no encouragement. He eagerly arrived at Lloyd's hotel room every night leading up to the fight, expending a ton of energy and an almost equal amount of semen fucking his opponent in every conceivable position, getting his cock and balls sucked and drained by both mouth and ass, until Washington finally left late in the night for that long ride back to the farm, clearly exhausted from the frantic sexual workout, with hardly any energy left for the following day's training session.

Lloyd, on the other underhand, only exhausted enough energy to get Washington coming—and coming, and coming. He kept his own vital juices bottled up inside. So that the following day in the gym, he tore into the heavy bag and his sparring partners with an animal ferocity born of sexual frustration and physical fight hunger.

His strategy was simple—and as dirty as it came: let The Natural do the heavy lifting in the bedroom, blowing out his balls and his legs and his stamina with all the sexual activity, thereby dissipating his strength, just as Lloyd himself had done so many times in the past during his stunted fight career. Lloyd guided the enthusiastic youngster's man-lust, unleashed it, but he held back on his own coming out party—that is, until fight night.

* * *

The temperature was over a hundred degrees in the outdoor ring that night, the humidity eighty percent. The Natural came out strong in the first few rounds, letting Lloyd have it with everything he had. But Pretty Boy held on, rubbed, rode out the storm, wily veteran that he was. And by the fifth round, Washington was already huffing and puffing, his mouth hanging open, gloves down, his legs lead weights that refused to carry him away from Lloyd's sharp, accurate punches.

Lloyd caught Washington up against the ropes in the tenth and pummeled him viciously, forcing the referee to step in and stop the fight. The Natural was out on his feet. He was fast asleep by the time they got him back to the dressing room.

DeSalvo jerked up his fighter's arm with glee. "We'll get more big money TV fights now for sure!" he bellowed over the roar of the crowd. "You were sensational!"

Pretty Boy Lloyd grinned, hardly a mark on him, his hard-on almost bursting his protective cup loose. "I could go another ten rounds—in or out of the ring," he boasted back. "But I'm going to go check on Washington. See if I can console him."

"Yeah, you go give that bum some tender lovin' care," DeSalvo jibed.

"Couldn't have said it better myself, boss."

APPETITE

Jordan Castillo Price

Jonathan tried to make a show of pouting, but he was lousy at it. Or maybe he was actually too good at it, because I was putty in his hands whenever he made that sulky little face. He tilted his chin down, let his dark hair spill across his eyes, and urged me on in that sexy Hungarian accent, saying my name with that sultry roll of the R. "Just try, Mark."

I sighed. It's not that I thought what he was asking for would be dangerous. Even with the small dose of aspirin he took, he was still a quick clotter. Quick enough that what he was proposing might not even work.

He sidled over to my desk and closed my laptop, which gave a mournful beep at being so rudely dismissed and then went into sleep mode. "Tonight." Jonathan's eyes bored into mine.

I had a feeling I wasn't going to get out of it, but I had to at least nod toward decorum. "Why tonight?"

"Because while you were up here writing, I've been getting ready."

This thing he'd been angling for—I hadn't realized there was any way to prepare.

But now we subscribed to all the V-magazines, even a lurid one from Germany, as well as the special subscription cable channels and the V-world website set as our home page. If a special preparation existed, Jonathan probably knew exactly how to go about it. I looked back at him and raised my eyebrows in expectation.

His long-sleeved T-shirt was a black V-fabric affair that hugged every chiseled contour. He pulled it up slowly, inch by inch, exposing his rock-hard abs, muscle after muscle. The tiny line of dark hair under his navel. His ribs. His nipples. I shifted a little but couldn't look away. He slid the shirt over his head, his hair momentarily trapped, then spilling down almost to his shoulders in a glossy, black tangle.

"Okay," I said. "You've got my attention."

His shirt dropped to the floor. He wet his mouth, and then trailed a fingertip across his chest.

"Look," he said.

I blinked and wondered what I was supposed to see. It was brutal, so much hotness, like staring into the sun. His paint-stained finger trailed over his chest, up his shoulder, down, languidly, as if he were modeling the wedding band he'd designed for us. But then I realized he wasn't showing off his handiwork—he was showing me a vein. I glanced up at his eyes and he smiled, satisfied.

"They're bulging," I said.

"Weight training. Don't worry, I was careful not to overdo."

I reached out to him, ran my finger down the vein he'd shown me, noticed everywhere it branched, connected, forming a whole network beneath his pale, translucent skin. And it turned me on, got me salivating, all at the same time. My god. I was drooling over the thought of what he wanted me to do. Damn him for his persistence.

"How long do we have?" My voice sounded dry.

"Plenty of time." He unhitched the buttons on his jeans with one hand and let the front fall open. His lower belly was a road map of veins.

My breath caught.

"See?" He sat on the floor and pulled me down beside him. When he shoved my hand down the front of his pants, I felt the bulging blood vessels, hard, pulsing and vibrant. "You like it."

My salivary glands continued working overtime and I had to swallow—and swallow again. "It's definitely . . . well . . ."

"Come on." He fell back. "I'm ready to be ravished."

He grinned up at me and used the tip of his tongue to toy with one of his fangs, causing me to wonder who was getting ravished, him or me? Not that I was complaining. My gaze trailed from his sinful, dark eyes, inching downward, enjoying every carved hill and valley, until I again came to those veins beneath his navel.

"I want you to bite my neck."

I felt a thrill that my puritanical brain tried to smother. "That's too dangerous." Okay, I know. Like anything was dangerous compared to surviving the ravages of the Human Hemovore Virus.

He pouted. Oh, man, what a pout. "My shoulder, then?" I didn't answer. He sighed and raised his eyebrows. "What is it? You want me to beg?"

"You beg pretty well; I'll give you that." I straddled his legs and buried my nose in his hair. It smelled like shampoo with an undertone of linseed oil and turpentine from his studio. "But no. You know I'm not into power plays."

Jonathan slid his hands up under my shirt and dragged his fingertips along my back. He wedged a knee between my legs and rocked his crotch into my thigh. Another wicked thrill—the way he approached it, sex, always flustered me and turned me on at the same time. The guy who'd once been unable to complete a successful pat on the arm was now humping my leg; copping feels in taxis; whispering dirty, dirty things in my ear at boring dinner parties where we couldn't eat anything anyway.

"Mark, fuck me while you do it."

My hands, as if outside my active control, grabbed his jeans by the front pockets and started tugging them down. Where'd he learn to talk like that in English—porn videos? I couldn't say things that crude. Not out loud. He twisted to dig something out of the back pocket while I stripped him, tossing the items on the floor beside us. A small bottle of lube and an X-Acto blade. I shivered.

He'd been barefoot, and once I got the jeans off, he just lay there looking up at me, naked, waiting. My gaze roamed his body. Veins showed everywhere, so much more prominent than usual, bulging over his shin, a pale blue web on his inner thigh. His hard belly, though—I couldn't stop looking there; it had me mesmerized.

I dropped my face to his stomach and kissed it. His hands went to my head and held me by the hair while he sighed, and I felt him stiffen against my collarbone. I dragged my lips over him, his fine, silky skin stretched over rock-hard muscle and bone—and now vein.

My salivary glands continued to pump as I took an abdominal vein between my lips, grazing it with my tongue. I could feel his pulse pounding, my heart stuttering as if to time itself to Jonathan's rhythms.

"Or there," he gasped. And he didn't sound so cocky anymore, pardon the choice of words. "You could do it there."

But it seemed a shame to waste all that good spit. Plus, he was sliding his hard-on along the side of my neck, so things pretty much handled themselves. I trailed my tongue lower, lavishing his stiff cock with attention while he panted and clutched my hair. I've told him to go easy on the hair, but he always seems to forget when I've got his dick halfway down my throat.

I had him nice and wet and all the way in, my head fixed between his hands while he flexed his hips upward, moaning. "Please." I tried to imagine us as we were back before his virus took me, a positive/negative blood-bond where the nourishment only went one way. I just couldn't picture it anymore, though. Couldn't imagine not kissing him, not touching him, not tasting him. More power to people who can live on flowers and poetry, but it just wasn't me.

I relaxed my throat and concentrated on the sensation of him sliding along the roof of my mouth, the faint hint of salty precome, the big vein I could feel rubbing against my tongue. Jonathan's hips dropped down to the carpet, but his hands stayed clenched in my hair. "I don't want to come yet," he said.

Normally, I'd keep going and figure I could always bring him to that point again, maybe even a few times over the course of the evening, but there was some challenge that appealed to me in choreographing the blood and the sex and both of our climaxes. He let go of me when I eased him out of my mouth. I gave the salty tip a final lingering lick.

I knelt up and looked at him, running my palms over his body while he squirmed beneath me, watching me with heavy-lidded, dreamy eyes. His veins still bulged, and I found my hands drawn to them, the sternum, over the shoulders, the base of the neck.

I salivated.

Nope, I told myself. Not the neck. Not without some big-time anatomy research.

And since when had the neck even become a serious option? One that turned me on?

Jonathan writhed under my hands and wet his lips while giving me a very plaintive, deprived look.

Suddenly, I realized I had way too many clothes on. I sent my Polo shirt flying across the room and unzipped my jeans, then shoved down my boxer-briefs. Jonathan tried to get his legs around me, but I flipped him onto his side, figuring I'd have better access to those veins in his shoulder if he weren't bent in half beneath me. He sighed and stretched as I got behind him, pulled his leg up before groping for the lube. "Touch yourself," I whispered, feeling like I was in a porn video myself, saying something so blatant. He purred a little and slid his hand between his legs, cupping his own balls, stroking them, while I in turn greased my fingers.

My fingertips brushed his when I reached down to lube him. He mumbled an encouragement that was mostly lost in breathing. I pushed a finger in—he was so incredibly tight that I felt like we were teenagers and not grown men. I had this suspicion that I'd been his first, at least that way, though it's always felt too awkward to really ask. "Do it," he begged.

I pulled my finger out and lubed myself up, stroking slowly, making sure I was hard, really hard. "Touch your . . . *dick*," I managed.

A breathy hiss, and I saw his arm change positions, his hand cradling it, stroking it for me.

I set my forehead into the curve where his neck met his shoulder and pushed a couple of fingers in, pressing toward the sweet spot. Jonathan moaned and arched his back.

"Come on, Mark," he said, rolling the R just a little. "Fuck me."

I pulled my fingers from his tight heat and lined myself up there, fucking my fist while the head of it poked at him, prodding, getting a sense of his body. He arched hard, backing onto me, and I let go of myself and took him by the hip bone, dragging him back harder. He raised a leg up, spreading for me, and with a final, well-placed thrust, I was in.

We both moaned.

Once I was inside—*so* damn tight—he dropped his leg back

down, tangling it between mine, his tightness becoming a glorious vise. A couple more thrusts and I didn't give two damns about the blood, just wanted that tight hole gripping me, stroking me, that hard body under my hands to take and taste and use.

Jonathan made the most exquisite sounds in his throat as he arched his back, pressing his rump into me, writhing in my arms. I crammed my forehead into his shoulder and felt sweat form between us, even though we kept the AC at a V-friendly sixty-five. I licked the salt of us from his shoulder blade.

"Now." He pressed a cold metal handle into my hand.

I didn't want to stop, but Jonathan had arched and held position with me pressed into him down to the balls. I took a shuddering breath and looked for a vein.

I almost went for a big one on the meaty muscle between his shoulder and neck, but opted for a little more caution, at least for the first time around.

First time? Like I could already see it as a recurring event?

I slid the sharp little blade under his skin and put my mouth to it.

Jonathan moaned, arched harder, managed to cram me deeper inside even though I'd thought I was as deep as I could possibly be.

A hint of blood, and the tiny cut closed.

"More," he panted in a low, gravelly voice, grinding his bottom against me. I could feel myself throbbing inside him, that final climb approaching.

I found that vein again by the tiny cut I'd made in it and once more slid the blade in, slicing the vein the long way, maybe a half-inch cut. I closed my mouth on it and sucked hard.

Jonathan cried out loud enough for the neighbors to hear.

It was only a little blood, but still, I was scared I'd hurt him.

"Come on," he panted, and thumped the floor with his fist for emphasis. "Really do it." His hand was moving fast on his dick, his breathing shallow, hitching. And I didn't think I'd hurt him at all.

My body seemed to agree with him, warmth gathering in my balls, my palms; the soles of my feet going all pins and needles. That big vein was right there, urging me on. The handle of the X-Acto was slick in my sweaty palm.

"Now." It sounded so strangled, and his ass throbbed around me as he said it.

A quick stick of the knife and I got my mouth on him and sucked. My insides exploded in a torrent of pleasure.

In retrospect, maybe it wasn't even the blood. It was Jonathan feeding me in his own moment of passion, and me drinking it, and the whole act escalating as it fed itself and fed itself, until it went nova.

I'd pushed Jonathan onto his face as I peaked, like I could pile-drive him into the Berber. His arms were trapped under him and his hair hid his face completely. I peeled myself off his back where I'd been stuck to him with perspiration, and saw his ribs rising and falling as he tried to catch his breath.

The cuts I'd made on his shoulder were nothing compared to the tooth marks around the biggest slice. A ring of red, straight lines for my incisors, with four black divots where my canines had bruised him.

Jonathan rolled onto his back beneath me and his cheeks were flushed, looking so fuckable I could practically go again. He nodded at me, as if to say, *See? I told you it would be amazing.*

I almost asked him if it had hurt, but of course it had. And then I told myself the question was probably irrelevant.

"Come here," he whispered, and pulled me down into a slow, gentle kiss. I shivered as sweat evaporated from my body, as his hand trailed down my side, settling low on my back.

When we broke the kiss, I stared into his eyes, even though we were too close to see properly. "Was it . . . *good?*" he asked. And not as a way of saying I-told-you-so—or at least that wasn't what I sensed.

Good? Lord have mercy. I nodded.

He let out a breath and hugged my head to the crook of his shoulder. "Then think about seeing the dentist and having your fangs sharpened. Don't say anything now—just give it some thought."

And wouldn't you know it, that idea sent a naughty thrill through me, too. I pressed my face into his hair. That was the price I paid for marrying the world's most notorious vampire. Just when I thought there was no other possible way to corrupt me, he managed to offer yet another wicked temptation.

FOURSOME

Gregory L. Norris

You tell yourself that you're not there yet. Far from it, actually. Eyes half-shut, high on the raw scent of sex between men, you spread your legs, which are bronzed from so many days working in the sun, and flex your foot. Warmth and wetness glide between the big toe and its longest, nearest neighbor. One of the three young men on the bed is licking that part of your anatomy. Normally, that would be an unthinkable act. Who in their right mind shoves his tongue on another dude's feet? In this business, you remind yourself, every visible part of a man's physique is somebody's favorite fetish, even—and sometimes especially—his size-twelve boats. It's all part of the show.

And, to your surprise, it's kind of a rush. You remember splashing in puddles on a lost summer afternoon when it rained and, somehow, the sun was out. You catch yourself smiling; growl out a happy, breathless, "*Fuck*."

The face down at your feet smiles, too. You forget his name. Rico? No, *Raul*. He ups the pleasure by licking slow, damp figure eights around the rest of your digits. To your left, the blond dude has already ascended to the prize between the other naked alpha male's hairy legs. The bed's a California King, but you and he—the alpha's name is Riley—you're sitting ass to ass, and so you feel his muscles tense, *swear* you can feel the suction of the blond guy's mouth on Riley's impressive cock, which matches yours in length, girth, and majesty. Same deal with what you both pack beneath your bones. Riley's balls are hairier. You trimmed yours a week ago—not for the video shoot, but because those long days in the sun painting houses make yours sweat enough without all that extra fur.

Riley's worshipper—Sam, that's his name—is amazing. Clearly, he loves what he's doing, and with his fresh face and athlete's body, you wish he'd spit out the thickness in his mouth and show yours a little affection. But Raul, apparently satiated on your foot-sweat, has begun advancing up your legs, licking you from hairy ankle past shin to knee, then thigh, and at long last reaching your balls.

As for Raul, if this wasn't some fly-by-night foursome taped for horny viewers to jerk off to the world over, you might ask the adorable, dark-haired imp who's happily enjoying your maleness out for a beer, followed by a repeat performance away from the pair of cameramen recording every detail. Yeah, you'd like that. In fact, you'd welcome the drink and the company of any of your costars on this crazy, unscripted story of two masculine alphas and the subservient beta males who worship them.

But back to the movie. Thankfully, you're not there yet, Logan. *There* being that point in a mainstream porn performer's career when he's squirted so much of his whitewash that the money shots are meager, a drop that amounts to pocket change, and the dude's balls have shriveled up, darkened in color, turned to shoe leather. Worse, rawhide. There are men in the business, you know from jacking off in front of your tablet, that look like they've got an iguana hanging beneath their tired dicks instead of scrotums.

That's not me, dude, you think. There's no spiny-crested lizard dangling beneath your root, where your balls used to be. This is a one and done situation, this porn shoot. Unless, of course, you get desperate again for the rent. Everything in this college town has gotten so damned expensive.

Your balls haven't shriveled and dried to desert, you notice, when you focus down on Raul, who's presently licking up and down the steely column of your shaft. Your nectar flows, proof of life. Your mind attempts to darken your mood again: what happens if someone recognizes you after this goes live? It will play forever across the Internet, saved to favorites and playlists and illegally shared long after DesperateCollegeJocks.com fades into history.

Maybe you'll finally score a decent date, the devil on your other shoulder jokes, and your smile returns. You'd like to date any one of these guys, even your fellow alpha male. Or shoot hoops with Riley at the basketball net in your driveway, where you mostly play solo games.

The two disciples change religions. Raul moves over to Riley, while Sam's mouth takes you fully, right on down to the balls. Riley moans and presses against you. You not only feel his arousal, you share in it. At one point, the other alpha leans his head on your shoulder. You experience the scrape of Riley's five o'clock shadow over your cheek at just after eleven on an overcast summer morning. Electricity crackles. The dude groans again. Not sure why, perhaps still thinking there's love here—brotherhood of a kind, at least—and you nuzzle against him. Riley faces up, and your lips connect. Kissing another male, especially one like you, a jock, an alpha, is nowhere near as questionable an action as you thought when you signed on to do this.

"Just see what happens," you recall the director with the deep pockets saying when he laid out the scene and offered you a cool thousand bucks to kick back, spread your legs, and have your body glorified. "Only do what comes naturally."

Lips crush together. Riley's tongue stabs at your teeth, seeking permission to enter. You grant it, and the sensation is nearly as powerful, as *wonderful*, as Sam's deep-throating of your cock. Riley's mouth tastes as good as any female's you've made out with. Better, because it's Riley. Natural. From somewhere beyond the tableau of the hotel room bed, you hear the director grunt in approval. Director? Such a generous title. He's no more one than you're a bona fide porn star, though, right about now, you sure feel like one of the brightest objects in the universe.

Riley: one of his arms is a canvas of barbed wire in ink, and what looks like a Chinese symbol. At that moment, through slitted eyes, his body art strikes you as rivaling that of the most famous works in all of human history. You'll never forget it, even after you've both nutted into the faces of Raul and Sam. They probably won't either. Riley's version of the *Mona Lisa* and Michelangelo's *David* and the first cave paintings done by prehistoric man will feature prominently in their future jerk-off fantasies, too.

Or maybe it's only *you* still holding on to the belief that this is somehow more, bigger than a paycheck, a job. Maybe it's a glimpse into what could be, not only for you but also them. *Shit*, your inner voice gasps, as your mouth does the same around Riley's in real time. How fucking awesome it would be to have *this,* not just for the time it takes you to shoot your wad, but every day for the rest of your life! You sure could get used to it. Riley as well, judging by the way he nips at your mouth in reaction to Raul's worship. He seems to want to capture your gasps of joy.

Wish in one hand, shit in the other, as your old man used to say—usually when insulting any of your dreams, crushing them more often than not. Happiness that runs so balls deep is impossible to maintain, and you feel it bubbling up inside you, starting at your well-loved toes. You spit out Riley's tongue, clamp your molars shut, and trap the howl as it powers up your throat.

Sam's expert attention to your cock's needs pushes you past the edge. Your entire body sparkles with the kind of energy and fire that first gave birth to the universe, only this Big Bang is on a cellular level. Sensing this, Sam draws Raul over, and both adorable faces savor your climax, their lips moving up and down either side of your shaft. The cameramen swarm closer—you've forgotten about them until they dart in to capture the first blast of your seed as it geysers between your worshippers' attractive smiles.

"Fuck yeah, dude," Riley sighs.

Through the rush of pins and needles and heat, you see his sexy grin, urging you on, giving you the porn version of a sporty high five in another kiss. It's that connection that does it for you more so than the smiles making your cock spit before gulping down your nectar. Riley's kiss. Oh yes, you sure could enjoy that in the days that make up the rest of your life.

Your wave crashes, but Riley's is about to start, according to his moans. Raul and Sam are kissing, their mouths wet with your seed. Riley's grunts alert them to his nearness. They scramble over and assume a similar position, with Sam leaning over your member toward the other alpha's. You clamp down on Riley's mouth with a kiss. He busts, struggling against your hug, a young man experiencing the best climax of his life, you wager. The two beta males lap, kiss. Your cock aches—not from being spent, no. Quite the opposite. It's still hard. Beyond stiff. It—*you*—crave more, more. A lifetime's supply.

Fresh sweat glistens on Riley's chest and arms. His ink and artwork do the impossible by becoming even more attractive. You struggle for breath, watching as Raul and Sam clean up the dregs. Then they're kissing while getting themselves off. One comes in his hand and licks his fingers. The other follows suit, and they kiss some more. The room reeks of manly sweat. Outside, thunder rumbles, as though to signal that the dream has ended.

There's more, sure. The director has all four of you jump off the bed. The quartet ambles into the bathroom for a shower, which, of course, will be videotaped for bonus footage. Raul comments on how hard your cock still is, even gives it a playful tug.

"Staying power, dude," you say, cool as January.

Inside, however, you're all tied in knots, beyond confused and burning up.

Riley runs the spray and gets in. You test the water and then follow. It's a big standup shower that easily accommodates four. This isn't really about getting clean, anyway. It's about the betas rubbing the alphas' backs with soap, washing their muscled butts, lathering up their crotches. Your cock is beyond ready for a repeat of what you enjoyed in the bed. This time, while the two worshippers worship, you lean against Riley and find him receptive, wrapping an arm around your furry waist as water cascades and steam obscures reality.

At one point, you boldly reach a hand behind you, seeking his cock. It's hard, too. You pump it with a few firm jerks, no longer worried about labels, only love—or the nearest thing to it.

Back in your truck, which is four years old and starting to show some wear, you've composed yourself. Your name is Logan. You work painting houses, which is backbreaking in the summer and scarce come November. You're employed by a dude who doesn't pay you fair wages for the amount of work you put in. As a boss, you'd do better, you often tell yourself.

You rent a house. It has two bedrooms, a private driveway, and a basketball hoop. One day, you'd like to own the place. You've never been late on the rent before—which is why you did a four-way with three other dudes. For all his degrading, your old man has never once taken into account how responsible you are when it comes to paying your bills on time.

It's a college town, with plenty of energy. You didn't go past your freshman year here, took the job painting houses. Given the turnaround of tenants, someone's always needing a room painted or a fresh exterior. You work hard for scraps.

Days after the shoot, your flesh is still electrified. Constant beating off won't keep your cock down. The warm, new summer breezes, scented of pinesap and humidity, leave you wanting, remembering. At the end of long workdays, you strip out of your sweaty socks and boxer-briefs and steal deep whiffs off them, imagining the scent as being Riley's. The bar of soap in your shower reminds you of Raul. While driving to the job, you pass a dude with blond hair jogging along Front Street and swear that it's Sam, though it isn't.

You paint houses, ponder, sweat, and recall. A week after the deed, you receive an email from the director—with a private link to preview the video before it goes live and an offer to do more work. A solo, maybe?

Solo, you think, shaking your head. You've had enough of being a lone wolf, and of being alone. While screening the video in the second bedroom—what passes for your man cave—your cock swells. Your nuts liquefy beneath it and hang halfway over the seat of the chair to your big, bare feet, which crave Raul's tongue. Breathing ceases being easy or even voluntary as you watch the action, aware of the bliss in your body double's smile. You marvel at how hot your costars appear, each one of them. And you think, *how many other porn actors feel this way?* That the sex they're performing is better than simple acting? It's *real*. You can't fake that level of chemistry.

Probably quite a few, the angel on your shoulder—it could be the devil—says. The industry is likely full of broken hearts and used condoms born of lust masquerading as love.

You jerk your stick, remember Sam licking you up and down, and Raul cleaning the hot, buttery stink from between your toes like it was a taste straight from Heaven, and how you played with Riley's maleness in the shower. That last notion unleashes a Fourth of July fireworks display that only you can see. Every atom and molecule in your body comes. You haven't even made it to the point in the video where you and Riley kiss.

A chill washes over you. You wipe your stroke-fingers on your sweaty T-shirt, reach for your phone, and text the director.

Need to talk, you type, and hit SEND.

He won't give you what you want—not their phone numbers, not even their emails. You tell him that you'll do more work, but only if he floats their contact information your way.

"Why?" he presses.

"*Nunya*," you growl and add, "*bizness*. That's the deal, dawg," you say, sounding so cool even as your insides tie themselves into knots.

You're at work, standing on the scaffolding strung across the second floor of a towering Georgian manor, when your cell phone vibrates in the pocket of your cargo shorts. The agitated ripples travel up your leg, tickle your balls, and tease the head of your cock. All the moisture drains from your mouth as your paint-brush stills. Reaching for your phone drags the seconds out with the weight of minutes. You don't recognize the number. Still, you answer, drawing looks from your fellow workmen.

"Yeah," you growl, your standard greeting.

In the pause that follows, your heart attempts to burst free of your rib cage or throw itself into your throat.

"Logan?" asks a young man's voice.

You'd know it anywhere. It's Sam!

The distortion in time deepens. In a disconnected manner, you're aware of telling him to hold on a sec, and of climbing down off the scaffolding like an excited kid on a jungle gym, cutting around the grand house to the driveway for some privacy, and of your instant erection.

"*Dude*," you emote, that dopey smile back on your face.

"I hear you're looking for me," Sam says lightly, and your smile widens.

You stand in the summer sunshine, growing harder, not sure of how to say that, yes, you've been looking for him and the others, that you asked the director to pass on your 411 to them. Then you see the boss's scowl, knowing you'll catch hell for this, and the words come to you with ease.

"I have a job offer for you," you say, no longer feeling like the hired help.

Raul texts you later that same night. You pace the rented house, expecting to hear from Riley—begging whatever power up there who might be listening that he'll call. Your phone rings, but it's a telemarketer. You tell them to remove you from their contact list and hang up before they argue the point.

You resume pacing, your erection metronoming in your shorts and underwear, complaining of its imprisonment.

Riley doesn't call. Ditto on texts and emails.

You were right about catching hell. The boss is a short man who drives a big truck and seldom does more than direct traffic. You've seen him pick up a paint brush, what, half a dozen times over the past four years since you started working for his company?

A warning? Seriously, for taking a phone call?

You paint angrily. There are six more houses after this job wraps, of which you'll get the leftover scraps once he's lined his pockets. Any time you feel your blood pressure begin to skyrocket and catch yourself grinding your molars, you remember that Raul and Sam are coming over after work.

You chill a six-pack of beer, put out chips and salsa, shower and change into a clean white T-shirt, jeans, and an old baseball cap with a frayed bill. You forgo socks, and for the second time in your life, you realize how attractive your big boats are after remembering the first time, when Raul was licking between your toes. Then you wait.

A hybrid pulls into the driveway. Sam bounds out, dressed in loose-fitting cotton shorts, ankle-length white socks, sneakers, a body-conscious polo shirt, and sunglasses. His clothes fit him in a way that should be criminal and makes you think they love his physique. As he glides toward the front door, you forget about acting cool and surrender to your joy.

"Hey, buddy," you say in greeting.

Sam lowers his sunglasses and enters the house. You draw him into your arms and hug, conscious that you're humping your stiffness into his. He catches on quickly and rewards you with an unapologetic squeeze. The contours of your living room, with its giant flat-screen and overstuffed sofa and chairs, dissolve in an effulgence of imaginary sunlight.

"I thought this was about a job," Sam chuckles and gropes your dick again.

"Yeah, it is," you say. "And not just a hum job."

But oh, the temptation to unzip is tangible, to shove your cock down his throat and kiss him after you shoot, tasting your seed on his tongue!

Another vehicle pulls into the driveway, a truck more beat-up than yours. You detach from Sam long enough to look out the screen door. You don't recognize it.

Raul exits the passenger's side. He's in shorts like Sam's, along with flip-flops that show off decent feet. The driver exits, clad in a ball cap, an old T-shirt bearing the logo of the local Major League baseball team, jeans, and sneakers.

It's Riley, and you smile again, because now the day feels complete.

"Look who I picked up," Raul says.

Riley laughs. "*I* picked up *your* ass, pal."

"The gang's all together again," Sam says, appearing beside you at the door, so close that you feel the warmth of his skin and smell the clean scent of his deodorant.

Yes, *complete*.

Riley eyes you once he's inside the house, his grin flashing a length of clean white teeth, the gesture more wolf's snarl than actual smile. He offers a tip of his chin, one of those typical greetings between alpha males that make instant buddies out of strangers on hoops courts and dusty summer baseball diamonds.

You extend your arms, and note the other young alpha's hesitation at meeting you in a simple bro-hug. A long second later, Riley embraces you. There's plenty of space between your crotches. You're not on a set anymore, you realize, and your happiness evaporates while clutching at a stranger. It was only a job to him, to all of them, your inner voice taunts. Just work, like any other labor done for a paycheck.

The dude-hug ends. Feigning cool, you invite your former costars into your home.

"Nice crib," Raul says.

You catch Riley gazing about. "Yeah," he agrees. "So why are we all here?"

"A job opportunity," Sam says. "I sure as fuck need it."

Turns out, they all do, which is why, like you, they found themselves sweating and moaning in a hotel room for DesperateCollegeJocks.com.

"I have an idea about how we all can make some green," you state. "I think it's a solid one."

"I'm listening," Riley grumbles.

You force your eyes over to his, and for the first time notice the depth of their blue color, like sapphires. There's something else in his bottled gaze, and it makes drawing breath almost impossible. Despite Riley's tough exterior, you sense the dude is being tormented in silence over the same confusion and desire that's left you walking around half-hard half the time, bone stiff the rest.

You smile, sigh. "Okay, here's my plan."

You invite them all to sit and lay out the thought: a second painting company in the college town, offering competitive rates. You took a year of business classes and know at least the basics about insurance and accounting. You'll need to invest in ladders and scaffolding, sure. But a few great reviews on social media and you'll be raking in the small fortune your boss presently enjoys, which only trickles down to you.

"All the company needs is a staff of hard workers," you say, both exhilarated at the possibilities and terrified that they won't hop aboard.

"I don't know how to paint," Sam says.

"There isn't a lot to know," you tell him. "You hold the handle like a pencil, firm strokes, feather the edges to stop the paint from clumping up."

"I don't mind working hard," Raul says, and you catch the mischievous glint in his eye. "Especially if it means being around hot painters all day long."

Sam chuckles and fires off an "Amen!" Only, it sounds more

like *ay-men* in this new bromenclature among fellow former porn performers.

Raul faces Riley, and for the first time you understand there's more at work between them. They rode over together. Friends? Boyfriends? Some hybrid of the two? Excitement rises from your toes and the temperature in the room seems to double.

"We clearly work well together as a team," you continue, ignoring the flush of arousal at what you believe to be the truth. "We could do this."

Riley shifts beside Raul. "And what about start-up capital? You sitting on some kind of trust fund?"

"No," you say. "But I know where we can land the cash to get things rolling. All four of us, we could come into the business as equal partners."

A few days later, the foursome is back in front of the cameras. Raul is servicing Riley, while Sam does this thing to you that no one has before: he's licking your ass with long, wet revolutions. The ecstasy is so intense that you worry you'll come not five minutes into the hour-long shoot. Then the paradigm shifts and the betas switch teams. Raul worships at your feet once more—a big hit with the DCJ.com viewership, you're told.

You find yourself shoulder-to-shoulder with Riley, growing higher on the clean male scent of his sweat and beguiled by the artistry of his inked arm. Moaning, the other alpha leans his head on your shoulder and, for a moment, you're back on the amateur hoops court in your driveway. It's the morning after the conversation in your living room, after pizza delivery, and after the hot four-way that took place in your bedroom. The mattress up there isn't as big, only your standard queen-size, but it still accommodated two alphas and an equal number of their beta admirers. Raul and Sam are still asleep. You've called out sick at work. You and Riley, both bare-chested and barefoot, toss around the basket-ball.

"I'm so new to this stuff," he says, the prickle back on his face, and looking so magnificent in the morning sunlight that you want to kiss him hard on the lips, not caring if the whole world sees.

"That makes two of us," you say lightly, nailing the next shot. Riley gains possession and dribbles. While pretending to focus on the ball, you steal looks at his feet. Big, sexy, in a way that part of a man's anatomy isn't supposed to be. He catches you staring and holds the ball.

"You really think this can work?" he challenges.

You take a heavy swallow before answering. "I do."

"I'm all for trying it, but . . ." he says, and sighs.

"What, dude?" He looks up, his brows furrowed. "Is it this other stuff?" you press.

Riley shakes his head. "Fuck, no. That's been keeping me afloat. Keeping me *sane.*"

He confesses to you that he's been living in his truck since flunking out of college, losing his scholarship, and pissing off his parents. The depth of his embarrassment and pain manifests clearly in those incredible blue gemstone eyes. Desperation, it's why he did that first video for DesperateCollegeJocks.com.

"If you hadn't," you tell him, "we wouldn't have met."

Riley's scowl cracks with the barest smile. At that moment, you realize how much you love him, this stranger you've only just met. But like the certainty that all four of you are puzzle pieces that fit seamlessly together, you're sure of this being genuine, too.

"There's plenty of room here," you say.

A kind of relief washes over his expression. "Dude, you sure?"

Oh yes. By the time you rejoin Raul and Sam, you've hammered out a nice little arrangement for all four of you to share those two bedrooms—one alpha and one beta per room. The deal is that you can switch it up as often as you like: you and Sam, you and Raul, and you and Riley, when the spirit moves you. And when all four of you opt to be together, well, you've already proven you can fit in your bed.

"We'll divide the rent four ways, and when we bank enough money, we'll buy this house," you say.

"Seeing each other at work and then at home," Riley says, "aren't you afraid we'll get sick of the company?"

You remember your loneliness, no longer stalking your days and nights, and how each of your new friends in this polyamorous foursome gives you something different, wonderful.

"I'm not too worried," you answer. It's easy to say, because you really and truly believe it.

You're back in the present, making out with Riley while Raul sucks your cock. Roommates, costars, coworkers—it strikes you that you've never been happier and look forward at last to all the joy your future promises.

THE TEMPTATION
OF THE GARGOYLE

Kyle E. Miller

Leviathan dropped from the saint's feet and joined the cascade of gargoyles at play in the open sky. He adored his brothers, loved to play hide-and-seek with them when the winter fog was up, giving them cover from the busy city below. They knew that a worshipper lifting his head to the sky before ducking into the dark of the cathedral would see only birds of prey. From their vantage on high, the city was a canvas of mist and damp macadam, straight city blocks suddenly warping to a blur as they capered and wheeled in the air. They gave chase in circles and figure eights, their cloud-bound world shifting, recreating itself all at once with each wild turn.

Rain came, as Leviathan knew it must, and the cascade returned to the cathedral to drain its roof of water and protect the mortar below. Rain was as close as they came to having blood. It was their calling and yet also their undoing. Rain would one day reduce them all to pebbles. But it was a slow death, so slow they might instead be demolished by other means first: an earthquake, perhaps, or the swinging of a wrecking ball. And for Leviathan alone among them, or so he thought, for he never shared thoughts this deep, rain was a pleasant death. He seemed always to be waiting for the next storm to tickle his wings with raindrops. It gave his whole body a tingle, and he relished in the ecstatic dripping of each drop, followed their paths as they lit his skin alive: along the smooth curve of his wings and down into the folds of his back; the nubs of the horns on his head and down across his face; his chest with its two tiny nipples, his stomach, his belly button and down, down, down. Where others saw only pitted wings and scarred brows, Leviathan saw the pattern of life itself. Water was a sensation. Water was erotic erosion.

Leviathan settled into place at the feet of the saint he thought of as his charge, now weeping tears of stone and rain. He wiped clean the backs of the bare feet and put his wings over them like a parasol. He knew those feet as well as he knew his own hands, and he tended them, he felt, not out of duty, but devotion.

And there was his neighbor, come home to roost, a rivulet of rainwater dribbling from his puckered lips. "Holy day to you, brother Leviathan."

Leviathan nodded, distracted by the gentle drops on his wing-backs, and muttered a reply. "Same to you."

"A good game today, yes? I almost . . ." But the gargoyle cut himself short. "What are you looking at, brother?"

Leviathan raised his head. "Nothing. It's nothing."

"I see."

"H'owlbear," Leviathan said to his brother, their names often as chimeric as their forms, "why do we never touch each other?"

"The works of the flesh are evident: sexual immorality, impurity, sensuality, idolatry, sorcery, enmity, strife, jealousy, fits of anger, rivalries, dissensions, divisions, envy, drunkenness, orgies, and others like these. I warn you, as I warned you before, that those who do such things will not inherit the kingdom of God. It's from Galatians, brother. Surely you remember Galatians."

"Yes. Galatians." The fog began to clear, and Leviathan could make out the shapes of humans far below. Red heads and blond ones, hatted heads and scarved ones. It was a Wednesday, he knew—gargoyles being born with the gifts of time—and his favorite day, the day his favorite human walked by below, the one he liked to watch. "And what about them?" He nodded toward the shuffling figures below. "Why do we not touch them?"

"Even more blasphemous," H'owlbear said. "They are not our charges. That would be to tread on the industry of God the Father. You know these things, brother. Has the rain reached your heart already?" For the gargoyle's gifts of speech, intelligence, wisdom, and truth are seated in the heart and not the mind, so as to be farther from the eroding rain.

"No," Leviathan said. "I just. I just—"

"Just what, brother? Enjoy the rainstorm. You'll find joy in your duty." H'owlbear puckered his lips and let the water flow, as if to say he had had enough talk.

And maybe it was the quality of the rain that day—a rain the gargoyles named *effervescentia* for its lightness, the almost buoyant effect it had on all it touched—but something woke in Leviathan that had been a long time dreaming. He felt it as a heaviness in the groin, as if it were made of some denser stone, something volcanic. He looked down again, always watching for the Wednesday man, and his foot slipped off the rain slicked perch. He saw from the corner of his eye H'owlbear chuckling as he pulled himself back up. He wasn't worried; a gargoyle always takes flight before striking the ground. The wings work of their own accord. It was impossible for a gargoyle to fall.

And wasn't that the problem just now, and every other Wednesday, when the man walked by below and he felt the pull of something greater than gravity, as if he were suddenly magnetized? Wings that worked on their own. Unless . . .

Leviathan waited until the next sunny day, when he was sure his neighbor and most of the cascade were sleeping. A crystalline winter day was not the time to caper about the cathedral rooftop or leave it entirely. They would be found out. But Leviathan was not going to leave, not yet.

He looked up at the weeping saint, as if to ask for forgiveness, and struck his wing against the cornice nearby.

Nothing can wake a gargoyle from his day nap, not the crunch of stone on stone, nor the crack of a broken wing.

Leviathan felt no pain in his wing that day, only in his heart, because he would never fly again. He had given up the sky for the Earth, and hoped the Wednesday man would come walking by again next week wearing no shoes at all, the only human he had ever seen go barefoot.

The next Wednesday night, Leviathan left his brothers behind.

His unbroken wing, still feebly pumping at the sky, slowed his descent, but everything in a gargoyle's heart is designed against the pull of gravity. They are born despising it, and the only thing preventing them from reversing it, or dying in the attempt, is that without it there would be no falling water and thus they would erase their own purpose, and, by gargoyle logic, their existence. The fall terrified him, and it was only when he reached the brick street below that he opened his eyes and breathed again.

The air was different down below. He had broken a talon in the fall. Saint James Cathedral looked massive and awful from a human's-eye view. No wonder they fell to their knees before its bulk. He didn't—couldn't—imagine what went on inside; the thought of entering a skyless space was still not in his heart. He felt small and powerless, and he wondered if humans always felt that way and if that was perhaps the cause of all their strife and warfare.

It would take getting used to.

"Hello?" he called out suddenly, without quite knowing what he was doing.

But there was no one about during the witching hour, and no one to answer his call. He was safe to explore the streets in solitude, free to put his feet on the bricks and walk like humans did. He was free to find somewhere to hide: a neglected dumpster, a shadowed corner, a heap of broken masonry.

He began to skulk into the darkness, avoiding lamplights. He never heard the footfalls of the man that came around the corner of the cathedral.

"Oh my god."

Leviathan froze. Perhaps there was still time to play as if dead, fallen by natural means. A slight movement might have been the trick of the imperfect human eye in the gloom of a moonless night.

"You broke a wing," the man said. Leviathan fought not to turn his head and look. *Was it him?* "You poor thing. How did you fall?"

He felt the man looking at him through the night and then approach. The lichens on his skin prickled. He felt the man's hands upon him, first on the nubs of his horns and then down to his mouth, over his chin, over the nipples, to the belly button. And then the man turned to leave, and Leviathan saw his bare feet and he cried out.

The man spun around, and something pulsed between them, a scent—petrichor, the smell of rain on stone—a look, a silent word, like the ghost of a rainstorm still hanging in the air after all the clouds have cleared. He was magnetized.

"Don't be afraid, my son," Leviathan said.

"I'm not," the man said. By lamplight, his eyes were the color of a midwinter squall. "Who are you?"

"I am the one who waited, son. The one who watched."

"So, it was you. I always felt as if, well, I thought it was stupid, but I always felt watched when I walked by here. That's why I come this way and not another."

Leviathan nodded, wanting to tell him that it was for him that he broke his wing, it was for him that he gave up the sky, but the words were all caught, turned to mud in his mouth.

"You looked a lot smaller up there," the man said. He was taller, but Leviathan was broader, bulkier, undoubtedly much stronger.

And the humans, Leviathan thought, had looked somehow larger. Not knowing what else to say, he offered the man his name.

"I'm Andrew." He lifted one of his feet to his hand and picked something from the sole, a pebble or a piece of gum. "Are you going to be all right?"

"I don't understand."

He pointed. "Your wing."

"Oh, I won't fly again, if that's what you mean."

"Can't you mend it?"

"What's done is done. Stone is struck. The commandments are sealed."

"Oh, well, I don't know anything about that, but couldn't you just . . . cement it back on? Or make a new one?"

Leviathan smiled, glad that the man for whom he had sacrificed flight had a mind and a heart, as well as two feet. "No, son. I'm not made of cement. If your arm fell off, could you glue it back on?"

Andrew chuckled. "I don't think that's quite the same."

For a moment, Leviathan was irritated by Andrew's nonchalance, and his pointed tail rose in anger. Didn't he know how serious this was? How careless this man was to treat it as a game. And yet, how could he know? Leviathan lowered his tail. He wondered what in the world of humans might compare to his descent. He was silent for a long time, so long he worried Andrew would leave, but he only stood there studying him. And then Leviathan had it. "It would be as if you were to suddenly descend into Hell from on high," he said. "I know nothing. I am no one here. This is another world to me."

"I'm sorry. I didn't know," Andrew said. He took a few steps closer and held out a hand. "But maybe I can be your guide through Hell."

Some early rising apostle chose then to practice his music inside the cathedral. Leviathan followed Andrew into the city and away from the creeping harpsichord of an ancient hymn.

Those first nights, Andrew took Leviathan on witching hour walks along the pier. They met in the dark. Leviathan found shelter during the day and slept, waking to the Earth world and wondering how Andrew spent his winter days. When they met and walked along the pier, Andrew taught him to see the ocean as he saw the sky. Leviathan loved the water, so vast and talkative, going nowhere it seemed. So deadly, he thought. Yet, wasn't this the stuff of his life? But there was rainwater and seawater, fresh and salt, and only Andrew could swim in the latter. Leviathan would merely sink, his wing less than useless, his life reduced to watching dropped anchors and coins tossed in for good fortune.

In their night walks, Leviathan learned that Andrew had come to the city alone. "With a black suitcase and nothing else," he said. "I am no one here. I know nothing." And yet he did. They both did, their knowledge never intersecting, so that they found each other endlessly interesting. Leviathan knew the names of every bird and their corresponding calls, had thirty words for water, could hear the inner workings of the Earth. Andrew knew about countries and borders, maps and legends, myths, and the folklore of long forgotten peoples. Their kinship was of mind as well as heart, soul as well as form.

One night, when Leviathan's clock of a heart told him spring was near, Andrew stripped to flesh itself and dove into the dark water, vanishing from the pier, indeed from all sight, before reappearing farther out to sea, a tiny head bobbing. He swam, kicking his feet at the moon, then diving down.

Leviathan's heart sank, but he knew Andrew would not. It was hide-and-seek in another medium, played the human way.

"Was it very cold?" Leviathan asked when Andrew pulled himself back onto the pier. He handed him his clothes.

"Thanks. Yes. Cold." His teeth spoke more than he did, shivering against each other. He was too cold even to dry himself, to make his limbs work. Leviathan began patting his feet with Andrew's shirt, and then, bright idea, he used his wing to fan the water away.

Andrew gave a cry of "Even colder!" and Leviathan began to dry him with his breath. The gargoyle's heart is a furnace, and each carries within himself a tiny Vulcan forging and reforging of the lambent jewel of his heart. His breath was hot and desert dry, a sweetness that touched Andrew's feet, ankles, calves, knees.

"My face," Andrew said, crouching. "Levi. My lips. Are numb." Levi, that was his pet name for the gargoyle.

Leviathan breathed on his blue lips and Andrew lost his balance or leaned forward—Leviathan would never know for certain which—and they touched. It was the forbidden, sacrilegious touch of lip to lip, open mouth to open mouth, and Leviathan filled Andrew with his own hot spirit, one long exhale that puffed out his chest and returned color to his lips.

It all happened so quickly: Leviathan was living in flesh-time now, not stone-time. Even with the rain and the weather, gargoyles were born to last. Humans, it seemed, were rushing toward each new pleasure, so as to experience as many as possible before they perished. They were driven by, and to, death. The time that followed that night on the pier was like the descent from the cathedral all over. He was falling again, only this time he hadn't jumped; he had been pushed.

They took turns worshipping each other's feet: the smooth tops, the calloused bottoms, the perfect plane of the sole, the toes and the creased spaces between. Andrew's feet were not like others'. They weren't as soft, since he had walked the world barefoot. The bottoms more closely resembled, yes, stone, tough and hard, and Leviathan spent days softening them with circular motions of his fingers. Every night was a massage that gave way to naked wonder.

Andrew came in the door and Leviathan was there, bent to the floor, removing the shoes he had to wear to work, undoing the laces, pulling them apart, slipping out a foot, and sucking, sniffing, licking the toes until he came: little crystals shooting forth from the tip of his pendulous cock, like fragments from the inside of a geode.

"Fuck me," Andrew would say, and Leviathan would fill him with his hot breath and finish undressing him. Though he was shorter than Andrew, his strength was much greater, and he would carry him to the bedroom and toss him onto the mattress. He slipped his stony fingers inside him. One finger, two, three, and then not his cock—not yet—but his biggest toe. One toe, two, three, and then finally the whole top half of his foot, in and out, playing at the small jewel of his prostate until warm pearls formed at the apex of Andrew's cock. They dribbled down and Leviathan drew them up with a finger and placed it in his mouth. He pulled his foot free and fell on top of him, pinning Andrew's arms to the floor, pulling his hole closer to his cock, his feet closer to his face. *Fuck me*, and he would, until Andrew came hands-free, feet-free, a perfect rivulet of opalescence strewn across Leviathan's one unbroken wing.

It dripped down to the folds of his back and lit him alive.

And, as always, in the afterglow, Leviathan thought of flight.

Leviathan woke from a dream about the center of the Earth.

He felt that the apartment was empty. They lived now in a hole in the wall of Old Town storefronts. Leviathan stayed there during the daylight hours, when Andrew was at work at a record store a few blocks away, when he rose early to shower, and Leviathan could sometimes catch him before he left, a few kisses on his feet. Leviathan napped heavily during the day, as gargoyles are wont to do, but when he awoke and Andrew was gone, he lingered in the places Andrew's feet had been. He found pillows Andrew's feet had rubbed against and put them to his face. He found blankets Andrew wrapped around his feet in winter and he draped them around his head. He hoarded socks and gathered shoes. He built an altar of the shoes Andrew was forced to wear to work and he masturbated, spraying them with tiny crystals that cascaded to the carpet.

Andrew came home, and Leviathan was at his feet. He wanted to live in the creases between his toes, cocoon himself in the sweet ripe smell, discard every rag of moss and fleck of lichen on his own body and replace them with whatever made Andrew's feet smell the way they did. He wanted to lie under the arch of his foot. He wanted to be trampled, stampeded, kicked. At times, Andrew found it difficult to walk around the apartment; Leviathan was always under foot. He would accidentally kick him and apologize, forgetting for a moment that his lover was made of stone.

Leviathan didn't know how many days or seasons he had lost to flesh, how many more he would lose. He delighted in every part of Andrew's body: the smell of his unwashed hair, the briny spice of his underarms, the fluff of his love handles, the curls of his pubic hair, the pillowy softness of his scrotum, so expansive and alive, so unlike his own tough little walnut shell.

Leviathan was beginning to forget, but just what he was forgetting he could not tell. Sometimes, after the candles had all extinguished themselves in pools of wax and they lay still in the dark, he wondered. Sometimes, he came close to remembering.

"Levi," Andrew said. "Levi. Levi?" He kissed the stub of his broken wing.

"Huh?"

Andrew chuckled. "What are you thinking about so hard?"

"Nothing, son. You."

"I bet." He kissed him again where he was the most broken. "Why do you call me son?"

"I—," but Leviathan didn't know. It was just there inside him, part of him since birth. Like all the other words (Latin, Greek, French), like time, like his heart. "It's just the way of things. Perhaps being above you physically, we—"

"The way of things," Andrew said, tugging on Leviathan's tail. "You were never one to obey, were you?"

"No." Leviathan jerked his tail free of Andrew's fingers and pushed him over, onto his back. "But you will obey," he said. "Open up to me, son."

One night, when Andrew was asleep, Leviathan crept out the door and into the street. He was surprised to find that it was warm, that it was summer, and he was ashamed to be so surprised. Had his heart stopped telling time? The days of their witching hour walks had long passed. He spent too little time outside and so much of it under a ceiling, cramped, suffocated. For an instant, he was irritated, furious, and he imagined raising welts across Andrew's back with his tail, hot red bands, each terminating in a triangle. He imagined him naked and battered, filled with throbbing stone, opened wide, again and again, until he pleaded, screamed for him to stop and let him come.

It was only when he reached the cathedral that he realized he had been walking.

He could see his brothers up above. Wasn't one of them just now taking a jaunt across the stars? His wings itched. Yes, both of them. He was just then conscious of his fallen wing, could feel it where it lay above. He was in two places at once, a fissure in his heart. New moss had grown on his dormant wing. He could feel the tiny emerald fibers. He remembered a saint's feet, now overgrown with damp and fungus. He remembered . . .

But no, he could not remember the reason. He no longer knew the reason of his birth or why the gargoyles congregated on the eaves of a crumbling cathedral.

He looked up once more before heading home, fearful of Andrew discovering his absence, ashamed at his earlier reverie, suddenly yearning for the warmth of human life. He looked up once and heard the haunting skree of some nocturnal bird.

Leviathan had forgotten the names of God, but he remembered the sky.

The clip-clip of cut toenails made a counter-rhythm to the rain outside the window. Leviathan always cut Andrew's toenails, taking each toe carefully in his hand and aligning each nail with the teeth of the clipper just so. He was proud of the perfect nails, proud because he had none of his own to clip. He had learned this just for Andrew.

When he was finished, he put the toes in his mouth. Andrew opened the window, filling the bathroom with the scent of rain. It tickled Leviathan's nostrils. His heart grew lighter, as if made of pumice.

"Outside," Leviathan said, and then he was carrying Andrew into the rainy night, his fingers slipping inside him even before he laid him on the tiny plot of grass behind the apartment. The rain on his wing, back, feet made his cock come alive. "Fuck me," Andrew whispered. "Fuck me, Levi." And first he used his fingers, and then his feet, nearly a whole foot this time, opening him up like a flower blooming pink in the rain, a blossom that was Leviathan's own to smell, to devour petal by petal, to lick the edges, blow on it like a dandelion and watch it quiver, so sensitive. There was more feeling there than Leviathan would ever sense on his stone skin. He marveled at the gap and then melted inside the heat of Andrew's body, a warmth as great as that caged within himself. Though this was a warmth all over, so much more profuse and complete.

When they were finished, Andrew playing with the crystals Leviathan had come, polishing them in the rain, Leviathan stretched out on his back and let the water wash the pebbles of his eyes.

"What are you thinking about?" Andrew asked.

"Nothing, son."

"It's not me. I can tell it's not me."

"What?"

Andrew let the crystals fall to the ground. "I can tell when you're not thinking about me. When you call me 'son,' especially."

"Oh. You know?"

He felt Andrew nod in the dark.

To think humans could be so empathetic, so willing to open themselves to others. Leviathan had underestimated them, or perhaps he had overestimated his own kind. Their thoughts and feelings were always so near the surface. He had thought of humans as diggers, burrowers, buriers, pushing everything they owned into hovels, burying their dead, always covering and concealing from the sky. Yet they left so much out in the open. They really were small and vulnerable, but not powerless, not at all.

It was a human, after all, that had called him to Earth.

And Andrew had been right; he hadn't been thinking about him. He'd been thinking about the stars, the sky, clouds, birds. Flight.

One night, Andrew came to him and said, "There's someone I'd like you to meet."

"What? Who?"

"Come on, get up, let's go."

"Why are you crying, son?" And suddenly Leviathan's heart filled with worry. Tightly nested in his adoration of Andrew, anything new felt like a threat. The threat of change. He recognized it from some moment long before, and his heart said *Let it happen*. He felt in it a cleaving, a gap he had been hoping to keep closed, one that could not be shut once opened, nor bridged. It was like the working of the plates beneath the Earth. Once the tremors began, there was only one way forward.

He quivered. He quaked like the leaves of the aspens Andrew loved in summer.

"I already told him everything," Andrew said. "He's a friend. One of the few."

Friend or not, Leviathan trembled all the way to the workshop, and when they arrived, he recognized the words on the lintel and the smells from within. They reminded him of home, of his early life, a deluge of nostalgia that struck him still.

"Come," Andrew said, taking Leviathan's hand in his. "Come on, Levi."

"No," Leviathan said. "Why? I don't understand."

"I want you to be happy."

Andrew led him around to the back where a man stood shirtless in the dust of a sodium lamp, back bent, giving birth to a pale marble woman reclining on a bench. The limbs of broken statuary littered the workshop floor.

"Levi, this is Antonio. I think . . . I think he can help you."

The world turned, as if Leviathan were once again in the sky playing games with the gargoyles, a blur of night and flesh and moonlit stone. Andrew's hand steadied him and then Antonio was stepping forward, slowly, as if approaching a wild animal. The clouds were falling, the fog rising, and Andrew was saying, "You don't have to decide anything today."

Leviathan, clinging to Andrew's moonlit feet, knew he already had.

CARJACKED

Kenzie Mathews

It was an inordinately long light, which is why I didn't notice I was being carjacked until it was too late. By the time I caught on, he'd kicked his foot down on mine and we were speeding along. I tried to play it cool, but the gun made me nervous. Otherwise, he was just the kind of guy I'd normally pick up: a dark, brooding bad boy. He had long black hair, dark hooded eyes, a white bone hook in his right ear, and a fire-dragon tattoo starting on the lower part of his neck. The tattoo curled southward into his black T-shirt. I figured there were several more under there, too. He had on jeans and black motorcycle boots. I ground my teeth. I wanted to fuck him so bad that it hurt.

Instead, I asked hoarsely, "Why didn't you kick me out?"

He mumbled something in reply. I slowed the car down. His boot stomped down on my foot again. The car sped up. He pointed in the direction he wanted to go. "You look like that guy, you know, in the movies . . ."

I practiced my yogic breathing. I *was* that guy, the actor guy in the movies. My carjacker looked at me, grabbed the wheel, and steered us to the side of the road. I gave up and braked. It came to me a little too late that I could've just hit the parked car in front of us and then made my escape. But if it's not scripted . . . well, I'm pretty, but not necessarily the sharpest crayon. Hesitantly, my eyes met his. He was grinning. His toothy smile was bewildering, stunning. For a carjacker, he was incredibly hot.

"You *are* that actor guy. They'll pay good money to get you back."

"I'm not," I said. "I'm his stand-in. Nobody will pay for me."

"No?" He picked up his gun and waved it around like a prop. "So why should I let you live then?"

I chickened out. I wanted to live. Be in better movies. Organize some charities. Talk more to my family. Make better choices, even in the men I'm attracted to. For example, no more dark, brooding bad boys with tats and piercings.

"Okay, I'm him. There's probably money for my safe return."

Bad boy grinned again and stroked my face. He murmured, "Money, even if you're returned *slightly used*."

I swallowed audibly. "Yes, even then . . . if something happened to me. If that was to occur, in the event—"

"Just shut up and drive." He laid his hand in my lap, cupping my thigh so that every dip in the road had that hand brushing my cock. I pulled back out into traffic. "Why are all the pretty ones so damn talky?"

I thought he wanted an answer. "I'm nervous, I talk when I'm—"

He gripped my thigh hard. "You're not talking your way out of this, Brandon. Can I call you Brandon? Like I said, *Brandon*, you do what I say, and it's all good for you."

"What if I don't want to?"

He leaned in, his breath warm on my skin, his lips brushing my cheek, "But you *do* want to, Brandon. You want to do everything I say so badly that your cock is tearing through your fucking jeans."

And that's when I realized how well he was handling my hard cock. He nodded his head toward a tiered parking lot. I pulled in and paid the attendant, my kidnapper publicly stroking my hard-on through my jeans the entire time. The attendant leered, but gave us a ticket for parking. We drove up until we reached the roof section. There were a few more cars up there, but no one around. I parked the car and waited, my heart pounding in my chest. I wanted to do this, but I didn't really want anyone to know either. I was supposed to seriously be dating Charlie. It's acceptable to have same-sex relationships now, but they don't want their gays to openly be dating other men on the side. Hollywood likes couples. Charlie and I had been open but quiet about it from day one. I liked Charlie, but he wasn't a bad boy. He was nothing like this bad boy, in fact, with his large hand on my hard cock, the one who put his gun on the dashboard as we sat there in silence for a few minutes.

I turned to him, opening my mouth to say something stupid. That's when he kissed me, hard. His tongue invaded like a Viking barbarian. His breath was musky masculine and his stubble scraped my smoother skin. Falling, dizzy, I kissed him back— tongue to sliding tongue, lips to crushed lips. He reached down and unzipped my pants and my cock sprang out of my jeans, throbbing, hard, painful. He ran his fingers up and down the length of it as I shuddered. He played with the head, and I moaned in his kiss. He started to milk it with a hard, definite hold, then softer strokes, with his fingers tickling and playing at the head. Hard and then soft and then playful again. My hips jerked with his motions. I grabbed the back of his head to pull him deeper into the kiss. He used both of his hands on me, one on my dick while his thumb caressed the head, the other rolling my balls.

I murmured, "Oh god," in his mouth. He pulled away, grinning. Then he winked at me and went down on my aching prick.

His tongue played with the head. He suckled, one of his hands on the shaft, holding me in place. His other hand continued to tease my balls. My hips danced, shooting my cock upward into his mouth, hitting the back of his throat. His hand started milking me, his tongue faster on the head. I came like rockets. He drank me, cleaning me up with his deft tongue. He then came up for air and gave me another dizzying kiss—sloppy, comfortable, with a little bite at the end. I tasted me in his kiss. I liked it. I liked him.

"You're going to call your agent now and tell him you need a few days to yourself."

"I'm not; I'm shooting in a few days."

"You are, because something came up."

I shook my head. "I can't do that. I have a career."

He took his gun from the dashboard and shoved it into the side of my head. Again, I realized too late that I could've taken the gun while he'd been sucking me off. I could've saved myself. But I hadn't. Maybe I hadn't wanted to. Maybe I wanted to drown in all this, tank my career. Maybe I'd needed to be kidnapped out of my stifling, restrictive, boring-ass Hollywood life. Maybe I'd bought the ticket, wanting to live the action instead of playing it.

"You *can* do it, Brandon, because I say so. Remember, *I'm* in charge of you now."

Each emphasis of his words got me a nice little push of the gun into the side of my head. I lifted my hands in defeat. "Okay, I'm making the call. You're in charge."

I made the call. Sy, my agent, was none too happy. I claimed mental breakdown. Sy said something about my career being fucked if I couldn't make it to the set on time, and I cried. I'm damn pretty when I cry, which is why I save it for the best scenes. Sy knew my work, but he fell for it, just the same. He let me go with an "I understand, kid." And it was done.

I sat there awhile with my cell in my hand. He reached over

and took it, then removed the chip. He threw it out of the car and nodded for me to drive. Once past the attendant and out on the road again, I said, "So, what's next?"

"We drive."

"Where to?"

"Wherever the fuck I want."

I started to feel frustrated. I guess Bad Boy wasn't up for dialogue or decent human conversation. "This isn't working for me."

He looked at me and started to laugh.

"What do I call you?" I said. "I have to call you something. Also, where are we going, so I know how to drive there. I need some answers, and I promise I'll leave it alone."

There was silence for a long time. I kept driving. Finally, he said, "Call me Jack. And how about Vegas?"

I nodded. "Jack. Vegas. Okay then."

I waited a bit, driving, leaving it alone, and then asked, "What were you going to do with my car?"

Jack laughed. "I was going to take it to some friends. Earn a little money. What do you think I was going to do?"

"Why are you like this?"

"Shut up."

"What?"

"Shut the fuck up and drive us to Vegas. From now on, I ask the questions and you answer." He turned his face my way. "Because I'm what?"

I didn't say it. He prodded me. I still didn't say it. He prodded me harder. I burst out, "In charge! You're the boss, okay? Jesus."

I waited. He didn't ask any questions. I turned on the radio. He turned it off. I drove. I waited some more. He turned on the radio again. I relaxed. Finally, after an hour, I asked, "What are we going to do in Vegas?"

His boot stomped down on mine and the car shot off faster.

When I saw the Vegas lights, I only had one thought. "Can we play the slots first?"

"First before what?" Jack smirked.

"Can we just please play the slots now?" I have an addiction. Bad boys and gambling. Booze never hurt, either.

"You have money, right?"

I nodded.

Jack said, "Well then, let's play."

I parked the car in a safe area and we started walking the Strip. Because nothing says fun like gambling in Las Vegas with your kidnapper. We hit the MGM Grand and Planet Hollywood. I wasn't recognized, which pleased me at first, because then I was really incognito and, for a change, not pestered by the paparazzi. Then I really thought about that, and it worried me instead. Not recognized? What the fuck? In any case, we went to Paris and got a room. We checked in under my name, with my credit card.

Yes, again, I could've screamed for help during check-in. There's plenty of security. But, honestly, I wasn't even considering it. I was thinking that it was kinda fun being kidnapped. I hadn't been hurt, plus the sex was consensual—and Jack was scorching hot. I'd had worse, more demeaning times on set. This was a piece of cake—and ice cream.

There was a couple in the elevator making out, a security guard behind us. I reached out and took Jack's hand. He snarled and flung my hand away. I looked at the mirrors and tried not to feel rejected by my kidnapper. The elevator doors opened and the couple got out. Jack took my hand and held it tightly. I was a little pissed he'd rejected me while the couple was there, but picked me back up the minute they were gone. And then I remembered that security was riding with us, which was possibly trouble for him.

So, I said to the security guard, "Rough night?" I didn't really expect an answer, but I wanted Jack to know a bit of fear. Jack tightened his grip on me. I smiled at him, a big, toothy shit-eating grin. He, in turn, stared at me for a while, then lifted our hands and kissed mine, his eyes never wavering from mine. The elevator mirrors reflected the three of us.

The guard's radio went off, someone speaking in coded numbers. He answered and then turned to us and said, "Another quiet evening at Paris. Enjoy your evening, gentlemen." The guard got off at the next floor. I didn't even notice. Jack and I were still staring at each other.

I spoke first; knowing what he was thinking. Mainly because I was thinking the same. "We can't."

Jack unzipped my jeans and tore them down. I had said we couldn't, but my dick had a mind of its own. Jack grinned at the sight and said, "Plenty of elevators, all running. No one will miss this one for a while." The door opened. He jammed his foot in it. No one was waiting—except for my hovering prick, of course.

He flipped me around so that I faced the rear mirror. "There are cameras in here."

Jack laughed, stroking my ass. "Since when are you shy on camera?"

I flushed. He had a point.

Jack reached down and started stroking the place behind my balls, just beneath my hole. I got harder fast. Jack smashed my face into the mirror glass. I moaned. He took a minute to get a rubber on and then he was back, one hand on my cock, the other sliding in and out of my spit-slick chute. One finger gliding in and out became two, then three, and by the time he slid in with the real deal, I was ready to buck out of my skin.

I rested my sweaty forehead against the cool glass, Jack's hand gliding up and down my hard cock all the while. My hips rocked with his as his cock slid in and out of my ass. Jack traced a line along the back of my neck with his tongue, biting me occasionally with every deep thrust. His other hand clutched at my throat, and I rolled my head back until his hand gripped my chin. Jack continued to thrust into my ass and bite my neck. I reached behind me and grabbed his ass, drawing him deeper into me, willing him in entirely.

We fucked faster, the sound echoing in the small enclosure and down the hallway. I was in that sweet place between pleasure and pain. I didn't want to be anywhere else. Jack's hand jerked on my dick. I thrust myself into his cock. Jack bit down on my neck. I exploded first and he came a few seconds later. I laughed as I came, as my aromatic load dribbled down the glass. I felt free, daring, rebellious. Yes, we were on camera and this could ruin my reputation, but I was fully satisfied—not to mention seriously fucked.

Jack pulled out and dropped the condom onto the floor. We rearranged our clothing, Jack now laughing a little, too, seemingly just as relieved as I was. I wanted to tell him I needed that, but I thought he probably already knew. I reached out and playfully pulled on his nipple. Jack snarled and shoved me back into the glass mirror. Then he jumped me, kissing me in that hard, definite way of his, as if claiming me, possessing me, marking me as his. I kissed him back, drinking him in. Our tongues clashed and wrestled. I sucked his lips as he chewed lightly on mine. We were oblivious to the world outside the elevator. There was only us and this.

Staring into my eyes, Jack said, "I already want to fuck you again."

I nodded. "You can do anything you like, for as long as you like, anytime you like."

"Because . . . ?"

I chuckled, "Yes, you're in charge."

His foot released the elevator door. Down we went.

Jack nodded and kissed me again. I fell hard for him and got dizzy. I found my way back by digging my hands into the back of his head and neck, bringing him closer to me. I wanted him to fill me again. I wanted him inside me, around me, with me, on top of me, beneath me, and beside me. I wanted all of him—brooding dark looks, dangerous edge, raging cock and all.

And yet, I pulled away.

"What now?" Jack growled.

"What happens next, after we fuck? Am I kidnapped or free?"

Jack stared at me, a serious look on his face. "If I let you go, will you leave?"

I shook my head and kissed him in reply. "No, I'm with you all the way."

Jack grinned. "Okay then, Brandon," he said as the elevator landed us in the lobby. "How about the Bellagio?"

I grinned back. *C'est la vie* Hollywood.

OPEN UP

Clare London

He hadn't been here before—I'd have remembered. I mean, I knew most of the names of the regular dental patients, but even if he wasn't one of the regulars, I'd have still remembered. I recognized what he was even though he was sitting in the waiting room in the middle of wailing children and white-faced youngsters and falsely cheerful adults. He barely looked up, flicking listlessly through a magazine. It looked incongruous in such large hands that were probably more used to manual labor. He grunted a couple of times—with impatience, I assumed, because we were running late. Now and then, his eyes flickered over a young man who sat opposite from him, and his shoulders tightened. I was probably the only one who saw it—again, because I recognized what he *was*. That is to say, what we both were.

It was the last hour of the day and I was kept busy through the remaining appointments. Gradually, the noise from the waiting room outside died away. Even my boss had gone for the day, but I offered to clear up the room for him. I just needed to wipe down the equipment with sterilizing wipes, refile some patient records, and run a swift mop over the floor—then I was free to lock up and go home.

I was washing around the sides of the sink when I felt the prickle at the back of my neck. When I turned around, I knew who I'd see.

He filled the doorway, leaning casually with one hand against the frame, the muscles bunching on his upper arm. It was a hot day and many people had left their jackets off, but I didn't remember him wearing one in the first place, just a white cotton T-shirt. In the waiting room, his bare, tanned forearms had been a visual oasis in the middle of striped dress shirts and pastel-colored dresses—his skin, glinting with sweat under the fluorescent lights. Now the T-shirt was creased and tight where it counted—right across his pecs. They were muscled and hard, straining the fabric across his chest. His nipples were tight button buds under the white jersey. I imagined that my fists could hammer on those muscles all day and never get an answer—except, of course, the one he wanted to give.

I cleared my throat. I resisted the urge to ogle him. "If you need to make another appointment, the girls can book you in tomorrow morning. We're closed now."

He didn't seem to be listening. His eyes were dark, set in a wide face and above a nose that had probably seen a fair share of action outside a boxing ring. His mouth was also wide, looked greedy, and was, of all things, grinning.

"You wear that thing for a joke or something?" His voice was slightly hoarse, maybe from too much smoking, maybe from the dry air in the surgery. Certainly not from nervousness. His eyes raked up and back down my body. Maybe they rested for a second longer than necessary at my crotch. I was glad the hem of my overall reached down to my hips, as I was suddenly hard. My hands clenched into involuntary fists and then opened out wide as if in surrender.

I bit back a whimper that begged to be released.

"It's my uniform," I said. It was a white polyester tunic, short sleeved, zipped down the front. Okay, so it was never going to be on the cover of *GQ* as this season's must-have, but it served its purpose. "It's what I wear at work." My voice sounded barely more than a whisper. The white, sterile walls of the room took its echo and swallowed it dead.

He shrugged, his whole upper body tensing then relaxing with the movement. The T-shirt rode up, exposing a small band of a belly that looked just as tanned and taut as the rest of him. His free hand came around to tug at the front of his jeans. He wore them fairly loose around the hips, though maybe that was less to do with fashion than to give enough comfort for thighs that looked strong enough to crush my hand if I dared slide it in between them.

"You can keep it on," he said.

"Huh?"

He took a step inside the room. His eyes flickered over the dental chair in the middle of the floor, currently set upright in its usual seating position. "Keep the dress thing on while I fuck you. If that turns you on, gets you hard."

My eyes widened with shock. "What the fuck? I told you, the surgery's closed for the day. You shouldn't even be in here. I'm locking up. There's no way—"

"There's every way," he said. It was amazing how he could do that with his voice—speak normally, with simple words, yet pitch the pure authority straight into my veins like a shot of drugs. I felt the pulse in my cock throb like a tangible squeeze. "You want it," he added. "And I give it. Head, hand job, dick up the ass, whatever. I got no time for games."

I flushed from head to toe. I took one step to the side, to keep the length of the chair between us. "Get out. I'll call someone!"

He shook his head. He was still grinning, and now his eyes

were fully on my crotch. One hand toyed with the button of his jeans—the buttonhole looked relaxed and loose, like it'd often been wrenched open in a rush. "All gone. They've all gone. Just you and me left."

"I have to clean up," I said, grasping for the first thing that came into my head.

"Let's get you dirty first," he hissed. "Drop your trousers. Get on the chair. Unless you want me to fuck you over the sink." He looked mildly quizzical for a second, and his hand cupped the bulge of his cock speculatively. "Or up against the wall. Those tiles slippery?"

I was still gaping at him, but the heat through my body wasn't just from indignation. No, my limbs were full of hot, spiking excitement and my heart hammered in my chest with joyous need. It had been too long since desire like this crawled through my veins, since it swamped me, drying my throat and filling my cock. Too miserably long! Too long spent in a quiet, single apartment; too long spent in busy, respectful days at work; too long spent with mild young men who bought me the occasional small glass of beer and wanted to talk about my opinion of current affairs.

"You looked at me," the man said.

I couldn't even nod. I realized I didn't even want to know his name.

"In that room." He jerked his head back toward the waiting room. "Couldn't take your eyes off me. So you're gagging for it. Don't make me hang around any longer." He moved his hand—large, bold, strong, with dark hair on the knuckles—and flipped open the button on his jeans. The zipper eased down swiftly, also clearly accustomed to his demands. There was something rosy red and swarthy behind his hand, nudging at his wrist, not cloth, not underwear at all. Hair. Skin. The hot, sweaty shadows of his cock, coming out to play.

"Fuck," I said, though I hadn't meant to say anything.

He laughed sharply. I didn't think it was *at* me, but then I didn't think he'd be interested in discussing the subtleties of humor with me, not right now, anyway. "Yeah. Get the chair flat and we'll fuck, like I said. You want it hard? It's going to be fast and I don't take requests once I'm started."

The last guy I fucked said I was too nice, said I was too submissive. To be honest, we both were, though I'd always thought there was something provocative in me that stopped me seeking that role on a full-time basis. Last guy and I ended up sharing a joint and watching reruns of *Friends* and never doing it more than once. Couldn't make our minds up how to do it a second time, then the moment passed.

I looked up at the guy in the doorway and knew that'd never happen with him. I doubted he had a TV in the bedroom. Hell, I doubted he used a bedroom all that often.

"Hard," I whispered. *Please* was implied.

He grinned again and stepped forward, pulling out his cock. I was fascinated by the purple-pink meat, which was thick, just as I'd imagined, the dark color a stark contrast to the icy white of the room. He smelled of musk. It jarred with the antiseptic tang in the air.

I stumbled around to reach the controls of the chair, winching down the back so that it could lie as a bed. I fumbled with one hand, trying to unzip my tunic, panicking whether I'd worn a clean undershirt myself today. My dick strained at the front of my trousers, trying to burst out. I knew they'd be stained damp before I finally got them open.

I also knew without doubt this was a one-off, limited-time offer.

The guy had moved forward, his jeans open but still hovering at his hips. He obviously wasn't going to get fully undressed, though he plucked the edge of his T-shirt and started to peel it up over his head. I'd get the top half naked at least, although I might never get to see those thighs, or trace the muscles in his solid buttocks curving inward as he clenched and thrust on top of me. My hole gripped tight, aching at the thought.

Suddenly, my foot knocked against the column under the chair and something whirred to life. He startled, his eyes widening.

"Hey." I lifted a hand, weakly. "Sorry. Just hit the foot pedal."

He'd gone pale—there was no mistaking it. He was starting to shake his head. He actually took a step backward. I stared between his dilating pupils and the thick, glistening cock in his fist, and I gulped in air.

"It was just the power. For the drills." I didn't know what else to say. My tunic was open, the seams flapping on my chest. My trousers were, indeed, damp at the front and clammy against my erection. In any case, I'd seen that look in men's eyes before, and it wasn't from sexual lust for my rather fetching ass.

"Fuck it," he said, frowning. "Turn the damned thing off."

I watched the flare of panic in his eyes. The power balance between us seemed to suddenly shift. My ambitions . . . well, they *changed.*

"Can't." I shrugged. "Something won't switch off. Maybe one of the connections isn't working." I ran a finger along the edge of the nearby unit, which was topped with a gleaming stainless-steel tray and a bright, white towel. "It's just the polisher. I've put all the loose instruments away." I glanced up at him and then back down to the tray. I had an irresistible urge to laugh. "It's only a noise." I tapped at the foot pedal with one foot and—apparently carelessly—folded my fingers around said polisher. It whirred for another second.

He moaned. I kid you not. The sound vibrated my bones.

We deal with it a lot in my line of work, the dental phobia.

Definitely more often than we deal with me being fucked raw on the chair.

I took a step nearer to him. "Are you scared? A lot of people are, when they visit the dentist, I mean."

"Fuck no!" His eyes were livid with a hideous mixture of lust, mortification, and fear. Irrational fear—yet very obvious. "I just had a checkup, didn't I? Fine with that—no problems there. You're talking crap."

"Okay." I shrugged. "Of course I am." I couldn't resist it—I tapped the pump again and the whine hissed through the room. The guy nearly went into spasm. He was struggling not to take flight—struggling to hang on to his pride and sexual credibility.

"You look pale," I said softly. "You should lie down on the chair first." You remember that provocation I mentioned before? The one that kept me just this side of submissive? Well, it was fighting now for my attention. "I really want you to fuck me. I really want it. *Now*." I shucked off my tunic and peeled my undershirt over my head. His eyes landed on my tight chest and thick nipples before glazing over, and his cock bounced in his fist, the color coming back to his cheeks. "Lie down," I said quickly. "I'll suck you."

It rested uncomfortably with him—me giving the instructions—but he sidled over to the chair and settled down heavily. The plastic cover wheezed under his weight, and the muscles in his belly tensed up around his navel. I stood close to the side of the chair, my heartbeat quickening again at the sight of him as I unzipped myself. I tucked my hands in the waistband and dropped both trousers and briefs together, letting them crumple around my ankles. My cock sprang out with its own version of hallelujah, desperation gleaming wetly and stickily at its tip.

His eyes flickered shakily between my modest offering to the prick party, and the central column of the unit—which wasn't the world's most flattering comparison for me—but I knew he wasn't viewing them from the same point of view. When I pushed the unit and tray to one side, he relaxed a little. Returning to the matter at hand, he prodded my thigh with the chubby wet head of his cock, gesturing it toward me.

"Suck it. Let me fuck that mouth of yours."

His hand reached up and tightened in my hair as he pushed me down on him—though I went willingly enough. I got a hand around the base of his cock before I gagged, and then I sucked as if I might never get another chance this side of the millennium. The shaft was so thick in my mouth that it needed all my attention. His hips thrust up against my chin, sweat springing up on that fabulous belly, my other hand clinging bravely to his hip to anchor myself. But when I crouched farther down to get a better angle on him, my boot again knocked against the unit. The chair creaked and the metal tray rattled.

I felt his answering shudder through his crotch.

I lifted my hand and put it flat on his stomach, holding him down on the chair. He grunted with irritation and tried to shake me off, so I pressed the edge of my foot properly down on the pedal and let the whine seep out—yet again. His cock jerked fiercely in my mouth and his torso went rigid. He stopped trying to push me off.

I grinned around his dick, my tongue licking fast. "Turn over," I murmured.

"Fuck off," he grunted. His conversation wasn't proving the most exciting I'd ever had during sex, but the circumstances rather limited us. "Your ass is the one taking it."

"Rimming," I informed him. "It's good. You want my tongue on your hole? Let me show you."

His cock throbbed on my tongue and he reluctantly slid it from my mouth. He huffed a bit and turned over, eyeing the unit beside us suspiciously. I kicked off my trousers completely, knelt up on the chair so I was straddling his hips, and then I tugged his jeans down his thighs. They were, as I'd imagined they would be, magnificent thighs. I ran my hand up them, feeling the line of the muscle, caressing the fuzz near the crease of his buttocks. I peeled his cheeks open, finding the dark, hairy pucker. I dropped a blob of spit down onto it, my saliva glands at full throttle at the sight of what was on the menu.

I guess I was simply clumsy in my excitement. Right? My foot slipped off the side of the chair and caught the edge of the unit, rattling the steel tray again.

The guy's body tensed all over, and so I got my view of the muscles of his ass after all, clenching in from the base of his spine down to the tops of his thighs. I sighed happily. He wriggled, too, though I was on top of his legs by now, my tongue at his crack. Maybe he was trying to get away—to restore his control of the situation. He liked it, though; I could tell. His hole flexed happily beneath my tongue's enthusiastic work, the pucker glinting with my saliva, the inside of his legs clenched tight with anticipation. I poked experimentally at him with my tongue, licking the rim as if looking for entrance. He grumbled from underneath me again. I rattled the tray again in response.

Suffice it to say, he went quiet.

I slid a hand in between his buttocks and poked a fingertip at his hole instead. He growled, and I had visions of being slung back off him, tumbling across the room, having to explain to my boss tomorrow morning why there were bloodstains on the tiling. But just as he was phrasing his by now familiar protest, my foot slid down over the side of the chair and caught the pedal. Full on, this time, and there was another burst of jarring whining from the unit. The air tube hissed as well, like it had come out in sympathy.

He went totally still. My hand was sticky with the sweat that sprang up on his skin. I went back to work.

I slid my finger in and out of his hole—it wasn't the hard passage I'd suspected, though every muscle spasm along his spine announced he hadn't expected this when he visited the clinic today.

"Just a checkup," I murmured, smirking. "Tell me if anything hurts."

"No way," he growled. "Get the fuck out of there."

I smiled, ignoring him, and slid in another daring finger. Like I said, it looked like he'd been here before. His voice was angry, but his knees pressed hard into the chair, and the corded muscles in his arms strained in eager anticipation. He lifted himself on one side and I could see the size of his swollen cock, trapped underneath his groin and begging for release. He was getting off on this, same as me.

There was the glimmer of foil peeking out of the top pocket of his jeans. With my free hand, I peeled out a condom packet. To fit all sizes. How thoughtful.

"Some of them have diamond coating," I said, cheerily. "The drills, that is. Makes them really hard wearing. And they have different speeds. Higher torque, smoother operation." I twisted my fingers, loosening him up even more, then fumbled under the tray, knowing what I'd find. "Lube for the hand pieces," I announced, my fingers suddenly very proficient with the one-handed opening of sealed containers. Amazing what proper motivation can do for you. "The drills can go up to 350,000 rpm. Adjustable forward and reverse." Newly slicked, I thrust in and out of him. When his back arched and his growls became fiercer, I knew I'd hit the right spot.

"What the fuck are you doing?" he panted. He sounded genuinely startled.

"Different kind of drilling," I muttered. I slid on the condom and slicked up my cock, my hand swift and steady, the flesh swollen and demanding. Then I pried open his cheeks again, tugging his hips up to meet mine. He came up onto his hands and knees, hobbled by the jeans still tangled around his thighs. His balls hung down in the valley between his legs, heavy and crinkled. His cock bobbed up from under his belly and he reached a hand around to grip it. I nudged my cock against his hole and pressed at the entrance.

He tensed again and swung his head around to glare at me.

I dropped a foot to the pedal and it whirred obediently. His pupils dilated, fast.

"Ask me nicely," I whispered. My cock throbbed in my hand, impatient to be balls-deep inside. I again nudged at him, his opening starting to relax around the head of my dick. When he hesitated—well, what do you *think* I did?

My foot tapped on the pedal. The whine settled into a much longer rhythm, an ululating wave of wailing. The tray rattled, the air tube sucked.

He keened, no other word for it. His yell echoed off the tiling and the white, clinical fittings like that of a trapped beast in heat. He clutched the sides of the chair and thrust his ass up toward me, pushing back onto my cock. "Fuck me," he groaned. "Get me out of here, but fuck me first!"

I guessed that was as polite as he was going to get. And one thing I know about phobias is that, allowed to run unchecked, they can interfere with normal functions—normal *bodily* functions, that is. We didn't want that to happen, did we?

I gripped his thighs and sucked in some air, hoping for more stamina than my excitement suggested was mine to command. I pressed slowly but firmly in, thrilled at the heavy, muscled body I had splayed out underneath me, taking whatever I had to give.

All he gave back, though, was a grunt, then a strange, wailing growl as I buried myself to my pubic hairs. His ass clenched around me and I groaned, too. My god, it was good! Tight, possessive, hot. I drew back, unpeeling my skin from the sweat on his butt, then thrust back in to the hilt.

The chair rocked beneath us, our panting steaming up the surrounding air. I felt I could do anything to him, could be as fierce as I dared. I was a young, hard, greedy stud! It was like pounding on—and into—a rock of flesh. *Magnificent!* My nails dug into his arms, my cock hammering like a piston. Months of unsatisfactory making out were wiped clean with this one, stupendous fuck.

Loud groaning. Wheezing breath. Creaking chair. That was us. *Me!*

He shuddered when he started to come, and it nearly unseated me. I clung on as best I could, my own climax uncoiling with a ferocity I hadn't ever experienced before. Goose bumps ran down my spine as heat flooded my crotch. One loud, embarrassing hiccup of excitement and my back arched, my head went back, and I sank as far as humanly possible into his ass. He bucked beneath me, his sharp cry bouncing off the sterile white walls.

My own ass tightened and the condom strained around me as I filled it.

Oh yes, so very magnificent!

Slowly, I withdrew and slid sideways off the chair. My legs didn't seem to be working properly and I sank embarrassingly onto the floor. I leaned my head briefly against the edge of the seat. A pulse throbbed gently in his leg, next to my cheek.

"Usually, you know, I don't," he said gruffly, like I was meant to understand. Which, of course, I did. He lifted a hand. Was he going to caress my face, run his fingers tenderly across my neck? No. He twisted a lock of my hair around his finger and tugged. *Hard.* The pain was surprisingly sharp.

I was ecstatic with it. My moan of pleasure may have given me away.

He smirked. "You wanna go again?"

I assumed the question was rhetorical. A glance at my hopeful dick already stirring against my thigh clearly gave him my answer.

He sat up on the chair, the plastic cover squeaking, his belly creasing above his crotch. He winced a little. "But not here. Near this . . . *stuff*." He gestured clumsily at the drills. "That was weird, right?"

I licked my lips and shrugged. "I guess it sorts the men from the boys."

He snorted. "You say that to all the poor fuckers who visit?"

I clambered onto my shaky legs, my discarded trousers in my hand. "Heavens, no. I usually have a far more reassuring line for them."

"Yeah?"

"Open up is what I say," I quipped. "This is hardly going to hurt at all."

BLADE OF GRASS

Vincent Meis

Camera in hand, lanyard dangling from my neck, I enter the stadium through the special entrance for the press. Someone shouts and motions for me to get down so I'm not blocking the view. I fall to my knees on the green grass and am quickly mesmerized by a close-up view of thirty to forty Turkish men, naked to the waist, olive-skinned and muscular, marching barefoot across the field, torsos glistening with oil. Their bouncy steps are in sync with the thundering sound of drums and the piercing wail of a wind instrument called a *zurna*. I immediately begin snapping pictures in rapid succession.

A few steps out onto the field, the wrestlers take a knee, reach down with one hand to touch the ground, and then in a quick motion touch their chest, lips, and forehead. They continue walking around the arena, find their designated partner, and begin the matches. I crawl in the grass as close as I can to the nearest pair. A referee waves me back to a distance that other photographers are respecting, and I wriggle my body backward while stopping every few feet to snap photos.

To arrive at this magical place, I only had to show my editor five minutes of a YouTube video about the annual Kirkpinar Wrestling Championships in Edirne, Turkey. My editor could offer me little in terms of expenses, but he enthusiastically embraced my project to photograph and write an article about it for the magazine. I imagined my friends from high school seeing my byline and being amused at the idea of me covering a wrestling event. In school, I felt pressured to choose a sport, and convinced myself wrestling would be a cool option. I suppose, deep down, it was just a desire for male contact. Big mistake. I was horrible at it. My weight group always pitted tall, skinny me with someone short and compact. Gangly against nimble, I lost every time. My teenage nickname, Beetie, didn't come from my red hair as many thought, but the way my face turned crimson from the effort of wrestling and the red splotches on my skin where I had been held and squeezed. Years later and with an adult's heightened appreciation of the male body, I stumbled across a video about Turkish Oil Wrestling. The mark that the wrestling nightmare had left on my brain was quickly erased, and I was soon on my way to the other side of the world to cover the event.

I am now prone on the field, shooting through the high grass. I try to block out the other journalists and the bleachers filled with fans, imagining that I am in the wild, as I was the summer before, on safari in Africa. I think of the wildebeests I photographed butting heads, as the two wrestlers touch foreheads and put their arms on each other's shoulders. They walk around in circles. One reaches out and grabs the waistband of his opponent. Since their bodies have been slathered with oil before the match begins, each participant is looking for a way to get a grip on his partner in order to flip him and pin him on his back. Another match on the field has already come to this conclusion after only a few minutes.

All the wrestlers wear leather breeches that tie at the waist, hang low on their hips, and reach down to their knees. In the back just below the waist, the leather is tooled and decorated with metal studs that spell out their names. In the match I'm watching I see it is Ibrahim versus Tarkan. Ibrahim has a mustache on a rugged but kind face; I'm betting on him.

Ibrahim gets a grip on Tarkan's waist and an intense struggle ensues, landing them both on the ground. Ibrahim is on top, but Tarkan manages to slip from under him and get behind him. Tarkan leans down on Ibrahim's back, crotch to butt, arm reaching under his chest to grab Ibrahim's left arm. Tarkan then changes tactics and slides his arm deep inside the waistband of Ibrahim's pants, wedging it along his thigh. I gasp. My camera goes *snap, snap, snap.* Is this legal? I look around at other pairs on the field and see that they are doing the same thing.

Muscles strain, positions change, the men emit grunts and grimaces. The sun beats down without mercy. After twenty minutes of constant flip-flopping, the two fighters suddenly stop as if by mutual agreement. They kneel and fall back on their heels. They stare into the distance, catching their breaths and wiping sweat from their brows. Blades of grass are stuck to their backs. And then Ibrahim's gaze falls directly on me, possibly drawn by the constant click of my camera. He tilts his head in question. A smile flashes.

The line of sight is then interrupted by a referee running over with a group of water and oil boys. It is a break. Each of the fighters stands up, takes a can of water, and pours it over his head, letting the water cascade over oily shoulders, down over glistening pectoral muscles and hairy navels before disappearing into the darkness of their breeches.

Then it is time to oil up again. For a moment, they are no longer adversaries, but comrades oiling each other's backs. I feel a pang of jealousy. The fight continues. My guy looks refreshed, while

Tarkan's energy is gone. Now it is Ibrahim who wedges his arm into the pants of the other, and with one swift motion, lifts him up and drops him on the ground, falling on top of him. The match is over; my guy has won. The referee holds up the winner's hand. The two fighters hug. Over Tarkan's shoulder, Ibrahim's eyes seem to lock on to mine again. His smile is now victorious. I still can't believe he is looking at me and I turn around to see if there is a wife or girlfriend in the stands. When I look back toward the field, they have left and joined a large group of wrestlers who have finished their matches or are waiting for their chance to enter the field. Many are sprawled on the ground, leaning against a chain-link fence, their arms draped over the shoulders of their fellows. Others are sitting in front of their friends, wedged between their legs, leaning strong backs against sweaty chests. I know when people see the pictures they are going to ask if they are all gay, and I will have to explain what I have learned in my travels throughout the Middle East (sometimes the hard way) that male affection, as endearing as it is, has little to do with being gay. I look for my guy. I have a fantasy of talking to him, turning the conversation to ask if he would model for me, knowing full well the words would only stick in my throat.

He has disappeared. I go back to taking pictures and spend the rest of the afternoon getting grass stains on my khakis. I see many examples of Olympic male beauty, but none of them interest me in the way Ibrahim did. That evening I walk the streets, gazing in the windows of every restaurant and café, strolling through hotel lobbies, looking for the smile that so captured me. Though I recognize many of the wrestlers, Ibrahim is nowhere to be found. I finish the night drinking too many beers in the hotel bar and get up late. I miss the morning matches. When I see Ibrahim walking with a towel around his shoulders toward the exit on the other side of the stadium, I realize I have missed his match and I bang my thigh with my fist.

The final day is filled with ceremony and medals and cheers and smiles. But I am hungover again, miserable, because Ibrahim is nowhere to be seen. If I could just talk to him a minute, maybe have tea with him at one of the little cafés, I would be completely happy. The event comes to a close and the exodus of wrestlers begins, back to their hometowns across the country, back to their mothers and wives and girlfriends. In hopes of running into Ibrahim, I have booked the hotel for one extra night and spend the morning hanging around the bus station until people begin to look at me suspiciously. Accepting my defeat, I rent a scooter with the intention of seeing some ruins outside the city, an Ottoman palace built when Edirne was the capital of the empire in the fourteenth and fifteenth centuries.

Going down a hill with a curve at the bottom, still thinking about Ibrahim and missed opportunities, I lose control and go off into the gravel. The bike tips over; I'm dragged along the ground, leaving me scraped, bruised, and in considerable pain. Luckily, I don't hit my head, as I'm not wearing a helmet. A good Samaritan stops and calls the police on his cell phone. He speaks no English, but sits with me on the side of the road. A long scrape along my arm is bleeding. He goes to his truck and gets a bottle of water, which he pours over my wound. The policeman arrives, followed by an ambulance. No one speaks English, but they understand the words American and photographer as I mimic taking pictures. I write down my name on a form.

At the hospital, the doctor speaks a little English and gets a nurse to clean my wounds. My T-shirt is ripped, dirty, and covered with blood. They take it and give me a hospital gown. They don't think I have any broken bones, but want me to get X-rays to be sure. A male nurse helps me hobble to a small building on the hospital grounds and deposits me in a plastic chair in an empty waiting room. He touches my strawberry hair and stares at me as if I were from another planet, his eyes like spots of coal framed by long, thick lashes. I try out the phrase I've learned for thank you, *"Te ekkür ederim."* He smiles as he puts the paperwork in my hands and leaves.

From the other room, I hear a man and a woman talking. A child is crying. The cry turns to a wail, a desperate choking sound. The woman's voice sounds agitated, the man's soothing. After a short time, the child is quiet. And then the woman in a hijab leaves the room carrying a small boy. The man calls out something in Turkish and I assume he is ready for me. He is sitting at a desk looking down at some papers. I notice his beautiful head of thick wavy hair and square jaw. He's wearing scrubs and glasses. I put the papers on his desk. He looks at them and then at me, startled. I'm still in the fog of pain and focus on the sweat that has soaked through the front and armpits of his top.

"Sorry. The air-conditioning is kaput," he says in excellent English. "And today of all days, the hottest day of the year." He stands up, takes off his glasses, pulls the top of his scrubs over his head, and hangs it on a hook. "I hope you don't mind. We are only men here now," he says, looking at the door where the woman has just left.

I am delighted by the face, the torso also unmistakable. I have gone through all my photos a dozen times and memorized the pattern of hair on his chest and the pleasure trail leading down from his navel. I stare at the little beads of sweat embedded in his chest hair. "Ibrahim," I croak.

He walks to his desk and looks at the papers again. "And you are Mr. Scott."

"Just Scott," I say. He takes my hand and holds it longer than a normal shake. He draws his hand away and touches his heart.

"You look so surprised. You think we *Pehlivan* have no life outside wrestling? We are not professionals. We must work."

He motions for me to sit on the examining table and goes behind me to untie the strings of my gown. "I remove this. I take X-rays, but first I want to see what I can see. Many times I don't need machines. I see or feel if there are broken bones. Please lie down. Oh, wait. Is better if you remove pants first."

"What?" I'm in a state of utter confusion, excitement mixed with bewilderment. I wouldn't normally be shy in front of a doctor, but I had photographed every inch of this man's exposed flesh, zoomed in on his face, and scoured every corner of the town in hopes of a glimpse of him.

He is amused by my hesitation. "Please," he says, helping me undo my belt and sliding the pants down over my feet. When the fabric rubs my skinned knee and I wince with pain, he grimaces in sympathy.

I lie on the table in my underwear. He begins his examination, putting his warm hands on the sides of my head, letting his fingers burrow into my hair. His crotch is touching the top of my head. All I can think is, *Please, God, don't let me get a hard-on.*

His hands move down to my shoulders, gently moving over my skin, pressing lightly. "You are very lucky," he says. "Your clavicles are fine. Very often, these are broken in this type of accident."

Next my arms. He covers inch by inch, kneading and prodding. I flinch when he gets near my arm wound. "Sorry," he says. And then my ribs, one by one. I'm ticklish and squirm a bit. He laughs before moving to my upper thigh. I use every ounce of strength to control myself. I think of cold showers and a dead rat I once saw covered with maggots. It's no use; there's a stirring.

"Are you married?" he asks.

I wonder if this is a professional question. "No. Are you?"

"Not any longer."

"Divorced?"

"No. My wife died in childbirth."

"I'm sorry."

"I have a daughter," he says with great affection.

Though perplexed by this personal turn, I want to know everything about him. "Will you remarry?"

"Why?"

"I mean, for your daughter's sake."

"Are you making me a proposal?"

Now, this is weird. He can't say that. He knows that I am enraptured, and he's playing with me. I try to laugh, but it hurts. "Ouch!" I say.

"In your country, this is possible for two men, no?"

I nod. There is a pounding under my ribs that feels like a beast trying to get out.

He finishes his examination and lays a hand on my arm. "Good news, my friend. No broken bones. I won't do the X-rays." He has a peculiar smile on his face. "But I want to try something else."

Sweet Jesus! This is not happening. I have fantasized about this man since the moment I saw him. We are alone and my hard-on rages inside my underwear.

"This maybe sounds a bit strange. Bear with me. Did you hear that the little boy stopped crying?"

"Yes, what did you do?"

"My grandma was a healer, gifted in the ancient ways. After my wrestling matches—I started when I was a little boy—she would put me on a table and do the passing of hands. It would take away the pain. Before she died, she told me I have the gift. 'But,' I say, 'you tell me the gift is only passed down through the women of the family.' She shrugs and says, 'Times are changing.' I think this is not possible. I study modern medicine at the university here and then in Amsterdam to complete my studies. There I learn my English. I want to know nothing of the ancient ways and I'm embarrassed as a man that my grandma thinks I have the gift. But sometimes, when people come to me in pain with broken bones, particularly children, I try the passing of hands. I find it works, that my grandma was right. So I want to try this for you."

I have reached my capacity for things I don't understand. "I'm good," I say. "I should go." I try to get up.

"Please," he says, putting a hand gently on my chest. "I only want to help."

In a few seconds, I am immobilized. Warmth spreads out from his fingers across my chest, up to my throat, and then down to my gut. My hard-on fades away, leaving only complete relaxation. I am sinking.

He puts his hands an inch or so above my solar plexus and slowly moves them to the top of my head, creating an aura of healing around me. By the third pass, I am out.

We are both in the stadium, now empty. The golden light of late afternoon surrounds us and falls on the grass, which is still glistening with the oil and sweat from the wrestlers' bodies. The scent of grass tickles my nose, triggering my allergies, and my body arches in preparation for a gigantic sneeze. Ibrahim's hand quickly goes to my chest and the sneeze disappears.

Oil leaks out of his fingertips and he rubs it over my torso. It drips down. I worry that it will stain my pants. At the same moment, I realize I wear no pants. I am naked, standing in the middle of the stadium where shortly before thousands of people had their eyes focused on this same spot. My next realization is that he is naked, too, standing close, radiating warmth, his hands now on my shoulders. He puts one hand on the back of my head, pulling my lips to his. We are pressed together, his chest hair brushing my nipples. I no longer try to control my arousal and I feel him growing, too. He lifts me up, and in slow motion we tumble to the ground, the grass a cushion, a bed. We continue falling as if going to the center of the Earth.

We roll over and over on the field, with blades of grass clinging to our bodies, now entwined in every position the wrestlers had previously assumed, wrapping arms, curling toes, sliding limbs, pressing flesh, not in battle but in a joining of bodies, of spirits. Tongues and lips explore. The taste of his skin is sweet and salty, with hints of oil. All boundaries have melted away. He is inside me and I in him at the same moment. Pressure mounts, bringing on our simultaneous explosions, our shouts of ecstasy echoing around the stadium. Aftershocks rock our bodies until we finally collapse into our joy and let our fluids—saliva, sweat, oil, semen— spill and drip onto the grass.

The sky turns rosy and the light falls away. We are looking up at the purple clouds, his arm under the back of my head. I hear his voice, but his lips don't move. "It will be with us forever." I don't understand his words. I am crying.

I open my eyes. My cheeks are wet. What I'm lying on is hard, not soft like the grass. The room is dark. I don't know where I am. I reach down and feel my damp underwear. I start to get up. "Slowly," a voice says. Then I remember the accident, the radiologist, the passing of hands.

I sit up on the edge of the table. "I was in another place."

"I know."

"You were there, too."

"Of course."

"I mean really there."

"I know." He turns on a low light and comes over to stand in front of me, a knowing expression on his face. On his right bicep, I see something, a dark streak that appears to be a blade of grass. I reach for it. It vanishes. My hand recoils.

"I have to go," I say. I stand up and look around the room for my pants. He puts his hands on my shoulders like he did in the dream or trance or whatever dark spell he put on me.

He pulls me into an embrace. My body stiffens. He whispers in my ear, "It will be with us forever."

"I don't know what that means," I whisper back.

"We don't have to understand everything my grandma said." He pulls back and looks deeply into my eyes. With his thumb, he brushes away a tear. I feel his power over me. "You have no reason to fear me, Scott."

"With this gift . . . can you . . . can you take people to another place . . . and do things?" I say.

"Only if both want it."

"Oh."

"How is your pain, my friend?"

It is only at this moment that I realize my pain is gone. I am grateful and filled with awe, but still unsure of what to think, caught in the twilight between reality and fantasy.

"I have no more patients and tonight I must go to my daughter. But first I take you back to your hotel, make sure you are comfortably in bed."

"It's not necessary." I pull away from him and put on my pants.

"Oh my beautiful red apple, you have traveled across oceans to a country and language you do not know, and you're afraid to go one step further?"

I don't know whether to run or weep.

"Take my hand," he says. "It is as simple as a blade of grass."

DIRTY TRICKS

Nelson House

"State Senator Nelson Jyles—we want you to set him up for a fall."

I leaned back in my chair, laced my fingers together, and stared at the dark-haired, hatchet-faced man sitting across from my desk. "That train wreck's going to smash into the station all on its own; what do you need me for?"

The guy didn't smile; he wasn't the type. "You in business as a hobby, Montreaux, or you want to make money?" He slapped a bundle of cash down on my desk.

Twenty thousand dollars. I'd quickly counted it.

Nelson Jyles was a three-term, born-again, conservative, African-American senator with an increasingly liberal lifestyle. His boozing had been a matter of record for years, but lately, aspersions of illicit orgy-play had been dogging the incumbent like a dark shadow. His hold on the Republican Party nomination was, therefore, shaky, his grasp on his senate seat slipping away like a spent cock out of a shot ass.

"I want to make money," I replied, honestly. "But where's all that bread coming from?"

The man leaned back, letting me fondle the green bundle. "Let's just say that some very interested parties with significant influence in this state don't want to see the seat change hands. Meaning, they want Jyles out, their new man installed in the primaries before the masses go to the polls."

I smelled the money and popped a boner. "Maybe the Stanton brothers, they the backers of this?" They, after all, were the richest right-wing wackos in our state.

The man stood up. He pulled a sheaf of papers out of his suit-jacket pocket and dropped them on my desk. "We'll consider you hired, Montreaux. This is the plan. Memorize it and burn it, and then see that it's executed. I'll be back to pick up the video."

I watched him stride out the front door of the building from my third-floor office window. He got into a cab, which pulled away from the curb, merging into the state capital traffic a moment later. I turned and again glanced at the wad of dough, the smile on my face as wide as the tenting in my slacks.

Senator Jyles liked to go for late-night jogs—jaunts, some would call them. They got him away from his security detail. He didn't think anybody knew about them.

The man who hired me, and that man's backers, certainly knew about them. As did a slew of reporters and capitol insiders, anxious to dig up enough dirt on the straight-laced-yet-straying senator, all of them eager to bury him. To be sure, it looked like Jyles was digging his own grave, judging by his erratic behavior of late.

Still, the wily politician was the leading, thundering voice of Christian right-wingism in the senate chamber. Not surprisingly, a good portion of the electorate liked that. His Democratic opponents, of course, not to mention the liberals in the media, hated the man. All that is to say, despite Jyles's impairments, he could still deliver the vote, both at the polls and on the floor.

In any case, the plan said he usually hit the trail behind the Capitol Building around midnight and jogged west down First Street, following the river under the Center Avenue Bridge. That's where we'd kidnap him, out of sight of anyone, so that he wouldn't have an alibi for the night.

I was at the wheel of the rental van when we finally spotted the senator slipping out of the Capitol Building, making a late-night run, five days after I'd been hired. I had three other men with me—operatives, let's call them. They didn't know the whys or the wherefores of the operation, just that they were to don alien masks and pick up a jogger, then hold him through the night at an isolated rural shack, releasing him in the morning. Nobody would get hurt—except, of course, the sleazy senator's re-election chances.

We tagged behind Jyles at a slow place. He was easy to spot on the wide, well-lit street that led away from the Capitol Building, but the farther he got from the dome, the darker it got. And when he legged it on down the sidewalk that curved just under the bridge, he all but disappeared.

That was our chance.

We slid the rubber alien masks over our heads. I gunned the van across Center Avenue, then skidded to a stop on the other side of the bridge. The three men piled out before running down the path to the river. I slammed the van into reverse and screeched back over the bridge, braked, then jumped out and jogged down the sidewalk the senator had just taken.

He was standing halfway under the bridge, my three men blocking his path. He turned and ran toward me. He abruptly stopped when he saw the glint of gunmetal in my gloved hand. A graffiti-scarred wall of concrete cut off retreat to his right, a rushing black river to his left. We had no trouble loading him into the van, binding and blindfolding and gagging him, then driving him out to the shack in the country.

The next phase of the operation was less tricky, though a whole lot dirtier. My client and his backers had located a man who was a dead ringer for Senator Nelson Jyles, right down to the streak of white that parted his black hair. I didn't know who the dude was, but he sure as hell had me convinced. And in the dimly lit confines of a seedy motel room, shot from a cheap pinhole camera, he'd soon enough have the entire state convinced.

The imposter Jyles and the additional three men I'd hired for the evening were all waiting for me in a room of the Boulevard Motel, a rundown joint on Front Street in the bad part of town. The other three men were prostitutes, all white. They were waiting in their birthday suits on the twin beds, along with the still-dressed faux Jyles, who was a handsome vision of ebony.

I made sure the camera up on the TV box was working okay, then stripped out of my dark clothing, baring my own brown body. I wasn't part of the main attraction, but I was going to star in the second feature; that was for damn sure. Every dick has to blow off steam now and then, right? Especially when somebody else is footing the bill.

I gave the thumbs up. The men, not to mention their hefty schlongs, swung into action.

One was a blond, one a redhead, the third a brunette. They all looked barely in their twenties, with slim, hairless bodies that looked like they would glow in the dark. They were as flamboyantly gay as you could get for two hundred dollars an hour, but their cocks were built adult-movie huge. I knew my city—and the men who worked, played, and lived on the streets there—and these three were perfect, just what the plan had called for. As to their real names, not a clue, but I referred to them as Zach, Darcy, and Allen.

Zach and Darcy helped the "senator" out of his clothes, as Allen hung a slender arm around the stand-in's broad shoulders and slid his long tongue in the man's mouth. The two men eagerly frenched as Zach and Darcy stripped away the senator's shirt and pants, baring the jogging-slim body of the debauched politico's double in all its stunning black glory.

I sat back in a chair in the corner and watched, polishing my erection to the pleasure of a plan coming together right before my appreciative eyes. The Jyles look-alike warmed to the action, sucking on Allen's tongue, thrusting his hips and cock out when the other two boys sunk to their knees and wrapped their white fingers around said black appendage, which looked more like a fifth limb than a cock.

They knew their dirty business, my guys, pumping out Jyles's cock to its full noir-steel length with their well-coordinated palms and wrists. Allen then filled the senator's open mouth with his tongue as Zach filled his own mouth with the senator's swollen cap. I jerked like I'd taken the wet, hot impact myself, imitating the reaction of Jyles's lithe body.

I leaned back and stroked with abandon, watching Zach's red lips flower over that knob and then flow down the shaft—his blond head and the senator's black hips tilted such that the camera could pick up all the action. Zach got himself a mouthful of cock, his downy cheeks bulging with dark meat. He then bobbed that pretty face of his, sucking delicious dick, moving smoothly and sensuously around it, all while Darcy played with Jyles's balls, fingering them, then dipping his red head down before sucking the black sack into his mouth.

Jyles's gleaming body spasmed again, his cock and balls getting the good old mouth treatment. He slurped on Allen's tongue, thrusting his hips to drive more of his cock into Zach's mouth. The action was hot enough to set any bent man on fire, incendiary enough—when surreptitiously released to the media—to incinerate a certain senator's career. Right-wing reactionary Nelson

Jyles never would get the gay vote anyway, but now he was certain to lose the Christian vote, too.

It would be a political career reduced to ashes—sooner, rather than later. Burn, baby, burn.

Darcy disgorged Jyles's sack and lifted his head up. Zach retracted his own head and fed Jyles's gleaming cock into Darcy's shining mouth. Darcy sucked on the hard length of meat, with Zach vaccing Jyles's heavy, slick balls. Allen dropped his head down and wound his pink tongue around and around Jyles's licorice nipples, biting down on them as the senator writhed and groaned.

Foreplay was fine, but we needed ass-fucking. I signalled with my cock. The boys shoved the sagging beds together on cue, then Zach and Darcy stretched out on their backs on top of the beds sideways, for best viewing. The senator climbed onto the bed in between them, on his hands and knees. He reached for one pink cock and pulled on it with his hand, then grabbed the other cock and pulled on it with his mouth, all while he waggled his taut bottom in the air like a black flag for Allen's hard-charging white cock.

I swallowed a moan, groping my nipples as I fisted my dick. Allen slammed his quickly sheathed and lubed cock into the sena-tor's dark hole and rammed it balls deep. All of the men on the bed groaned out loud, the star of the show just about choking on Zach's cock as his hole got pummeled. Allen gripped Jyles's waist and pumped his hips hard and heavy, fucking our man's ass in no uncertain terms. The senator, it seemed, didn't just like to give cock, he liked to get cocked, too. And there was no way that would go over well with his constituency. Still, I was enjoying it—and I was in the majority in that sordid little room of ours.

Allen bit his lip and tilted his head back, churning Jyles's chute. His thin white thighs smacked against Jyles's tight black cheeks, setting them to quaking as cock cleaved asshole. Jyles urgently blew one dick, then the other, fist-pumping the slickened one he wasn't sucking. The beds creaked and the fetid air funked with sweat. I gritted my teeth and pulled on my prick and twisted my sack, dripping sweat from my forehead and armpits, cock raging and balls boiling.

But there was still more staged drama to play out—and all of it hardcore.

Everyone in the scene got a shot at Senator Nelson Jyles's ass. Allen pulled out with a sticky pop and Zach plugged in. Jyles sucked Allen now, his body rocking to the beat of Zach's long, hard cock reaming his rectum. I added more lube to my own wood, so that I wouldn't get splinters.

It went on like that for ten minutes or so, my boys and the backers' chosen one exhibiting plenty of stamina to go along with the passion. Still, we needed a good climax to this skin flick of ours.

And so, the three white boys lined up in a row of asses on the bed, all of them on their hands and knees, hot pink holes one after the other. Standing up on his own knees from behind, Jyles plunged an inviting anus with his now-rubbered cock as he banged to and fro, then unplugged and long-corked the next steamy opening in line, pile-driving that hole for all it was worth. Up and down the row of asses he went, the guys urging him on, drilling one chute and then the other and then the other before starting back at the beginning again—until even he couldn't take any more.

It was then that Jyles let out a howl of pure, perverted delight and blasted one hot load into that rubber and Allen's ass. He then quickly ripped his spouting hose out of Allen's tight hole, tore off the latex, and sprayed first the backside of Darcy and then of Zach, until come dripped down from everywhere.

I stood up with one hand on my cock, waving with the other,

directing the final scene. The three men tumbled off the beds and up onto their feet, crowding around Jyles, who was now down on his knees on the threadbare carpet. The senator leaned back against the bed, his head tilted happily up and his mouth hanging hungrily open, a look of absolute pleasure on his chiseled, dark features, watching as the threesome jacked their shiny, surging cocks directly at his face.

Allen exploded first, blasting ropes of hot sperm down onto Jyles, painting the gleaming black face with white steaming streaks. Then Darcy and Zach jerked together, letting loose their torrents of come, coating the senator's face just like he'd coated their backsides.

With shaking fingers, I stepped forward and shut off the camera, then shoved my way through the naked, spent men and plunged my cock full-bore into Jyles's open, dripping mouth—past his come-drenched lips and deep into his come-clogged throat. I roared and went off like a cannon, blasting burst after burst of my soul-shattering load down the man's gulping, greedy throat.

I mean, why should they have had all the fun?

It all started to unravel by the time I drove out to the shack in the country to secure the actual senator's release. There was a posse of men there ahead of me, professional detectives from an international agency with a good reputation. They had possession of the shocked-looking senator, all of them standing before the amassing TV cameras. Rubber alien masks were strewn about on the grass in front of the shack. I shifted gears, hightailing it out of there, smelling a double-cross like shit on my shoes.

The real scheme was fully revealed later that day on the news. My sex tape was played—heavily-censored, of course—all while the senator commentated, calmly and commandingly now, explaining how it couldn't be him in the video because he had a large purple birthmark on his right thigh and the impostor in the video clearly didn't. It was a setup, you see. The good senator's political enemies had kidnapped him and shot the incriminating video, all in an effort to discredit the man and ruin his re-election chances.

I sat back in my office chair and shook my head. It was obvious, at least now. My black-haired, hatchet-faced friend and his backers wanted Senator Nelson Jyles to remain in office for as long as they could manage him. It was damage control taken on the offensive. Dirty tricks so dirty even *I* felt a little used.

MINISTRATIONS

T. Hitman

I suppose the hug that night was meant innocently enough. Farnsworth Sutton—or Skip, as we called the youth pastor of the First Baptist Church of Salem Limits—had stripped down to his tightwhites. I remember thinking, despite having swallowed lightning, how magnificent his underwear fit him, as though it loved his body. Also not lost on me was the gap along the inner leg, wide enough so that I could steal glimpses of Skip's balls hanging big and meaty and covered in dark blond fur.

God, how I loved Skip.

The previous summer, I'd turned eighteen, which meant this was my last youth retreat. It also meant I couldn't bunk with the other youths, and so I was bunking with Skip instead, which felt worth more than the entire universe to me. What had started out as a teenage crush had traveled far deeper than my epidermis, my blood, even my marrow. The emotion, now entrenched in my very soul, bubbled up from that distant realm, unleashing pins and needles through my flesh that were equal parts icy and hot.

"Skip," I somehow managed.

He turned from the second bunk in the attic room of the Western Slope House, a sagging Victorian structure rising up from the trees on Mount Major, perpetual home to youth groups and other religious retreats. From the cut of my eye, I'd been admiring Skip's butt, one of those perfect asses, more square from well-worked muscles than round. I thought of all the times I'd watched him playing hoops in the church parking lot with the jocks, so consumed by want I was sure I'd spontaneously combust from the heat. The back view was magnificent. Up close, the front threatened to blind me, like staring directly at the noonday sun. Skip Sutton *radiated*.

In quick order, I drank in his image: dirty blond hair in a neat cut, summer blue eyes behind glasses, and a mustache that routinely conjured my lustiest dreams. He stood at the six-foot mark, an inch or two taller than I. His body was one of those lean, perfect columns, with a line of dark blond fur cutting him down the middle of his torso, hairy athlete's legs, and big feet. He was only five years older than me, and yet it felt like centuries.

"Yeah, Curtis?"

For a terrible second, I forgot my reason for invoking his name. The way he spoke mine made me love him all the more. "Just wanted," I shrugged, "you know, to thank you."

Skip absently scratched at his junk, the temperature in the attic bedroom instantly doubling, driving out the edge of October briskness. "No need, dude," he said, smiling that crooked, sexy smile that made me crave his kiss. "I'm glad we get to hang one last time."

His words dumped a bucket of imaginary ice water over my joy. The last time? With summer at a close, school done with, I was working a lousy nowhere job, unsure of what to do with my life. The only thing I was certain of was what I felt for Skip Sutton. I caught a hint of his male scent on my next desperate sip of breath—a mix of clean sweat, the dregs of deodorant slapped on hours earlier, and something more, something magical. Only later would I realize it was Skip's arousal, his testosterone working up through blood and skin.

"No, I meant . . ." I struggled for the words. "For everything. You know, all along."

Skip's smile widened. He extended his arms, an action that stirred his manly scent. In a daze, I walked into his hug, loving the strength of his arms, the heat of his naked skin against me, the safety of his embrace. With my head buried between his bare shoulder and neck, I savored the warmth of his breath as it poured down on me, stoking both my happiness and concern. My last retreat. Going forward, I wouldn't be part of Skip's youth group, the one true joy in my life.

I sensed his thickness pressing against me. I was so focused on that one detail that I at first missed others, like how his big, bare feet formed an outer wall around mine; how he held on, his hug lasting. I never wanted Skip to let go. And now, it seemed, he wasn't letting me go.

My heart galloped. I imagined it throwing itself against my ribs in an effort to jump out of my chest and into my throat. Sucking down a desperate sip of his manly scent, I boldly reached lower. Skip tensed as my fingers gripped the bulge at the front of his underwear.

"*Curtis,*" he moaned, speaking my name as though it were the most powerful component of a sermon or prayer.

Nearly paralyzed by fear and emotion, it took me another moment to realize that, as our hug had continued, so my hand was still on Skip's cock, and he made no move to stop me from fondling his maleness. I dipped my pinky into the hole in his underwear and gently tickled his balls. Some unaffected register in my racing thoughts recorded Skip's swallow near my ear, what sounded to me as dry, from a throat suddenly full of invisible hot coals. The hardened state of Skip's cock confirmed his excitement.

He sighed my name again. "This is . . ."

"Wrong? I know," I said, and pulled my hand off Skip's tantalizing thickness.

He chuckled, a sound that had always unleashed flutters in my stomach. "I was gonna say *incredible.*"

I lifted my head. Our eyes connected, my pedestrian browns with his dazzling summer blues. In that bottled gaze, I saw what I believed—and hoped—was joy. Then, wonder of wonders, he cupped my face in his hands and crushed our mouths together. We kissed, and my flesh was reminded that ice can sometimes burn and that heat can make you shiver.

Skip. Magnificent Skip. The invisible centuries that had separated us had suddenly vanished, and so I sank to my knees before him. Skip grunted a throaty, "Yes," which to my ears sounded holier than *amen.*

I pressed my face against his crotch and inhaled. Skip's musk filled my lungs. I breathed in another hit and instantly grew high on his scent of hair, sweat, balls. My fingers scrambled for his elastic waistband. Skip's cock spilled into full view, a column at its thickest state, with a mushroom head and the fullest pair of balls hanging down below, all of it wreathed in luxurious dirty blond fur.

Skip gripped the back of my head and guided me forward. My lips met his tip, which was only just beginning to leak nectar. The tang of his precome ignited on my taste buds. My right hand gently tugged on his heavy balls; my other caressed the hairy muscles of his leg. More of his turgid cock entered my mouth.

I sucked, and the man of my dreams began to rock on his feet, thrusting into me.

Dreams? Surely, this was one and nothing more—the most vivid of my inexperienced and young life. At eighteen plus a handful of months, I had little to compare the experience to, apart from secret, private fantasies, most involving the very man whose cock I now worshipped. I knew to open wide, to avoid teeth, to let his willingness determine how aggressive I was with his balls. That part of Skip's anatomy appeared to like my increasingly forceful yanks. At one point, I spit out Skip's cock and focused my new sucking skills on his balls, loving their smell, their taste, their round fullness.

No, this wasn't a dream, I realized, aware of the joy on my face, the fresh sweat on Skip's when I gazed up, the red rising from the top of his chest to stain his throat and cheeks in rosy arousal.

"Suck it," he rasped. "Suck my cock, Curtis."

I spit out Skip's left ball and happily obeyed. Not long after that, his erection seemed to expand in my mouth. Skip huffed out a breathy string of expletives, and then the first blast of his seed painted my tonsils. I mentally counted the next half dozen while swallowing to keep up, recording the salty, sour taste, loving it as much as I did him.

When Skip's climax subsided, he stepped back and pulled his still stiff cock from my mouth. Drawing me up to my feet, he again kissed me, his tongue swabbing his own spilled seed off my lips. Saying nothing else, Skip pulled me into his arms and then his bed.

I didn't believe in all that Old Testament nonsense about a God who hated the notion of men loving other men more than violence, murder, and warfare. I told Skip that as we spooned together, our fingers laced, his reawakened cock pulsing against my bare ass.

"All that really matter are the red letters," Skip whispered in my ear. Our fingers tightened. "His only commandment was that we love one another."

The words trembled up from my guts in the darkness, made it onto my tongue and almost to my lips. But before I could tell Skip that I loved him, he chuckled, and my insides again caught fire at the sound of his glee.

"Besides, I was never keen on that Old Testament mentality— blood sacrifices, slave ownership, and the like," he said. "And I have to admit, I enjoy a good lobster roll from time to time, even though eating things that crawl in the sea is considered one of those deal breakers to getting into Heaven."

Tears welled in my eyes as he hugged me even tighter. I felt loved. As though sensing this, Skip leaned in closer and kissed my throat. He continued to hump against me, igniting a craving in my core for a different, deeper form of contact. The next moment passed without words, through a kind of telepathy.

Skip released me. His breath scattered over my naked spine, along with short, hungry kisses all leading down toward my ass. I panicked, tensed.

"It's okay," he soothed. "Trust me."

I did. His hands spread apart the halves of my ass. His tongue entered me first, then his pointer finger. Certain that I was going to come apart from the intense sensation, a mix of pain and plea- sure, I gave myself to him, trusting Skip as his quickly sheathed cock filled me fully, the gonging weight of his balls telling me he could go no farther. Skip drew back, and the darkness before my eyes erupted in an explosion of supernovas that only I could see. He slammed in, the universe recreating inside me.

All at once, my discomfort vanished and all became pleasure. I imagined us as a yin and a yang, a circle completed.

The words at last powered past my lips. "I love you, Skip."

Though I couldn't be sure he heard them through the cacophony of moans.

As I eventually drifted off to sleep, I was certain that nothing could kill my happiness.

Sadly, I'd been mistaken.

Kevin Sweezy and I weren't what you'd call friends, but we did attend youth group together. At the First Baptist, in the big function room where the group met, we were holdovers from summer, permitted to be there, but likely not for much longer. Kevin and I sat together at a table.

It was ten minutes past the normal start of youth group. My entire body felt alive, as though every cell was smiling in anticipation of seeing Skip. Then Pastor Dunne, an older man with a barrel chest and a big nose, ambled into the room.

"Listen up," he bellowed. "Effective immediately, I'll be your new youth leader. Pastor Sutton is taking a leave of absence."

My soul separated from my body. I listened, not believing the words, aware that my mouth hung open but lacking the means to close it. Skip gone? Why? How?

Then it struck me—*the retreat!* What if someone had found out about our secret love, and reported it to the church elders? Nobody had said anything to me. Even so, guilt put Pastor Dunne's narrowed eyes directly upon me, accusing me of unforgivable crimes. It was only paranoia, I told myself, my mind attempting to convince my body, the two halves still split apart. The icy-hot pinpricks slithering over my flesh spoke otherwise.

"I hear it's because he's run away with some woman from town," Kevin Sweezy said only loud enough for me to hear.

My soul slammed back into my body. "No," I fired back. "That isn't true."

"How would you know?" he huffed.

Pastor Dunne's eyes found us. He coughed to clear his throat.

"Sorry, Pastor," Kevin said.

I fumed, my lips finally clamping shut. How did I know? Because he wouldn't do that to me, couldn't. Could he?

Excusing myself for a bathroom break, I continued straight down the corridor and pushed open the big wooden door. October dusk brooded outside. I stormed out of the church into a chilly night, which was redolent with the crisp fragrance of autumn leaves, and walked away.

I plodded down the sidewalk, head held low, fighting back tears and, at first, succeeding. If Skip was gone from the youth group, did that also mean he was done with the First Baptist? A leave of absence? For how long? Though none of that mattered at that moment. All I knew was that the one good thing in my life was now gone.

Tears welled up. I'd learned what it was like to be with the man I loved, thinking he loved me in return. Now I knew the scope of what I'd lost. The tears soon powered past my ability to contain them. I made it over to a crumbling rock wall and sat down, allowing the salty drops to spill.

It could have been minutes or hours later when the rusting black pickup truck pulled close to the curb. I wiped my eyes, but wanted to cry for an entirely different reason. The truck was Skip's.

I stood and hastened over to the passenger side door. The window powered down. Skip sat behind the wheel, a reassuring grin beaming on his handsome face.

"Get in," he said.

I opened the door and took to his side, happier than I could ever recall being on the heels of the most despair I'd ever suffered. He drove away. To where I didn't care, so long as we were together.

Salem Limits passed beyond the windshield and windows. Under the threat of gathering rain clouds, the desolate quality of our surroundings struck me again. Without Skip Sutton, the town would be unbearable.

He reached his right hand over and captured my left, raised it to his lips and kissed. "How are you, Curtis?"

I was better following his arrival; that much was for certain. "I'm fine," I said, and truly, I was.

He kissed my hand again. I wiggled my fingers free and boldly reached between Skip's legs, groping the bulge at the front of his jeans. Skip moaned and permitted my exploration. At one point, he pulled onto a side street I didn't recognize and, in the darkness at the edge of the curb, I went down on him.

"*Yes*," Skip sighed.

I leaned up to kiss him, sharing his nectar as we had on Mount Major. He lapped at my mouth, and his enthusiasm at taking his body's seed stoked my lust.

I loved Skip, and confessed so once again.

Skip's smile returned. With his cock still exposed and the terrifying silence between us growing as I held on, hoping for him to declare those same three words, he stroked my cheek with his thumb.

"Curtis," he said, "I love you, too. In fact . . ." He righted in the driver's seat, stirring the wonderful, sweaty haze we'd conjured. Skip faced me directly, his eyes projecting a look that was all business. "I, uh, I guess you heard."

"About the youth group? Sure."

He reached down and stroked my hand. "I'm leaving First Baptist for good, leaving this town, too." His words challenged all the joy swirling around inside me, ironing the happy smile off my face. "I'm leaving it all for you, actually." That chuckle of his rode like wildfire down my spine. "Come with me."

Suddenly, thinking and breathing weren't possible. "With you?" I gasped.

"I've found an apartment. It's small, and money-wise, things'll be tight at first, but you can take classes at night at the local community college, and there's a job I'm looking into, and—"

"Yes," I said.

We kissed again. Our lips parted, and the storm clouds drifted apart enough so that the full October moon's radiance could envelop us, like a sign from some higher power celebrating our unexpected and divine love.

OUT OF YOSHIWARA

Wayne Goodman

Usagi Uchikina looked left, right, and behind him before tentatively stepping from the Nihon-Zutsumi embankment onto the
bridge crossing over to Yoshiwara. As the eldest son of a great
shipping magnate, he had to be careful not to be observed going to
the Floating World for his pleasure. This was the first time he had
actually set toe upon the slender causeway connecting Edo to the
island of forbidden delights. His previous attempts stopped short
of crossing when niggling fears overcame compelling desires.

*Who might see me? Would anyone recognize me? Will I shame
my father and his company if someone knows I have gone to
Yoshiwara?* His thoughts agonized between maintaining the good
face of his family and satisfying his ever-increasing urges to be
intimate with another man.

Had Uchikina been born with the interest in women that most
other men had, he would not have had to resort to such stealthy
behavior. He'd heard there were other men who felt as he did—
and that he would probably find them in Yoshiwara—but as
the eldest son, and obvious heir, to a powerful merchant of the

Kitamaebune Northern Sea trade, he did not feel secure enough to make public his particular preference for male companionship.

On the right side of the path he noticed a wishing well. Uchikina quickly tossed a few *mon* coins for good fortune and hurried to the entry gate. He kept his head, his needs motivating him forward.

At the gate, an old woman stopped him with her tiger gaze. Back bent, tattered silk embroidered jacket nearly touching the ground, she spat, "What do you want?"

What do I want? The question is expected, but the questioner is not. How can I explain? Uchikina hesitated.

Dark brown spittle dribbled down her wrinkled chin. Again, she hissed, "What do you want?" The timid man looked all around, and then peered into the face of the guardian of pleasures as she wiped her chin with a sleeve. Her eyes opened wide, like new moons. Her cataracts clearly reflected the light of the lantern overhead. "Usagi-san?" the woman asked warily.

How does she recognize me? Uchikina pondered. *I am wearing peasant clothes and the pilgrim hat worn by samurai to conceal their forbidden visits to the Floating City.*

Uchikina nodded carefully, barely moving his head.

A wise smile crossed the old woman's face. "You want a nice, young lady?" she goaded with a wrinkled smile.

No, not a woman, he thought. He shook his head slightly. "A man," he whispered.

"Well . . . a male geisha it is." She nodded, touching a bony finger to her nose, then turned and began walking into the walled city. After a few steps, she turned back and motioned for Uchikina to follow.

No tipping, please. Uchikina read to himself. It was a sign posted on the pillar at the first intersection. *How strange. If one is to receive excellent service, tipping should be essential.*

They walked past two main lanes that intersected the path.

Along the way, paintings on the walls displayed people engaged in sexual activities, many of them forbidden back in Edo. At some of the paintings, men sat with their robes open, pleasuring themselves while studying the enticing artwork. Seeing other men touching themselves aroused Uchikina and caused a noticeable bulge to form at the front of his gown.

"Wait!" barked the old woman. "You must wait!" And she slapped at his crotch.

She wants me to wait. For what? Have I made the wrong decision? He contemplated running back to the safety of Edo, but before he could move, the scrawny old woman grabbed his wrist with unexpected strength and pulled him toward a door a few paces off the walkway.

After knocking gently, the woman slid open a small panel at her eye level and whispered a few words. She stepped back and pointed to the opening.

Uchikina stood, unable to move, paralyzed with fear.

The bony woman grabbed him by the wrist and pulled him up to the door, again pointing through the small opening. When Uchikina dared to look, he saw a set of beautiful eyes looking back at him.

These are pretty eyes, decorated with alluring paints. "Is that a man?" He turned to his guide.

She nodded curtly and responded, "Yes, that is a male geisha." Her smile revealed browning teeth beneath leathery lips as she nodded again.

He is a man, but his eyes appear quite feminine. I wonder if this is the one she has picked for me. Uchikina pointed to himself, his eyebrows raised in question.

The woman nodded with a knowing grin. "You will now attend the tea ceremony," the woman whispered.

Tea? thought Uchikina. *Such a strange custom.* "Fine," he agreed.

"And you must pay for the tea!"

Uchikina sighed. "Fine, fine. Can we please get on with this?"

The old woman sneered and led him to a different room. She slid open a rice-paper wall panel and indicated for him to go inside.

Uchikina peered in and saw four ornate pillows around a small table. *I shall be having tea with my geisha tonight!* He walked inside and sat on one of the pillows. The woman smiled, bowed, and retreated, closing the panel behind her. Around the room on various tables sat bonsai arrangements, cinnabar statues, incense burners, and ivory lamps. Hanging on the wall he could see scrolls of poetry written in elaborate characters. He breathed in the heady scent of the incense, prick throbbing.

A few minutes later, another panel opened. Through the entrance stepped a beautifully adorned figure in a purple silk kimono, with the distinctive flat red cap of pleasure bringers resting atop layers of loosely braided hair with dangling strings of cherry blossoms, and delicate feet clad in white hose on tall, oval-shaped bamboo *okobo* slippers. The ceremonial bow was performed so deeply it looked like the geisha might drop the tea tray and topple from the elevated shoes. Jasmine-scented steam suddenly filled the air. Uchikina's head swam.

The geisha placed a small porcelain cup on the table, filled it halfway, then picked up some nearby peach blossoms, smiling ever so slightly as they were attached to slender wrists. Uchikina looked up at the geisha with a blank expression. *That old woman must have misunderstood. I do not want a female geisha. This was a bad idea. I must leave. Now!* He stepped toward the door, but the geisha jumped in front of him and urgently pointed to the tatami mat on the floor.

Uchikina stared at the authoritative figure and shriveled inside. Weak and impotent, his head hung like a drooping plum, wilting under its own weight. He couldn't even walk out of a tearoom under his own volition. *Failure!* he thought. With no further resistance, he sat on the floor as directed.

A fan appeared from within the robe's sleeve as the stranger began to dance, undulating in precise motions: a hip thrust, an arm lunge, the opening and closing of the fan, a tilt of the head. The tassel hanging from the fan swung around like a fish on a line and Uchikina followed its hypnotizing motions with his eyes, not knowing what to do in this uncomfortable situation. *I will have spent my father's money for nothing!*

The fan disappeared back into the sleeve and the figure moved toward him, pushing him down onto the mat in a sitting position. Uchikina reluctantly allowed himself to be ordered around. He felt his hat being removed, and when the bare skin of a hand touched his neck, an unpredictable swelling began again. As he landed on the mat, the hand caressed his ear, the swelling continued.

Why am I aroused? This does not make sense! His thoughts raced.

Two hands now rubbed his shaven crown, stimulating the bare skin. *I am enjoying this! Why?* When the geisha gently pulled on the topknot, audible sighs escaped from the quivering lips of the now-terrified man.

With his eyes closed, Uchikina imagined a man touching him in this manner. While it was not specifically sexual, it was still very exciting. Just as he began to picture the face of his young page boy, something hit him in the nose.

He opened his eyes to see a bulge in the front of the geisha's kimono. Instinctively, he reached up to touch the protrusion, but his hand got slapped away. *Is the womanly figure before me actually a man?* Uchikina looked up into the face of the other and asked, "You are a man?"

The geisha nodded in the affirmative. That explained why Uchikina found this intimacy arousing. His geisha was a young man, after all! An almost imperceptible stain began to form inside his *fundoshi*. He was leaking now, his cock clearly eager.

In a rare act of self-disclosure, he pointed to himself and said, "Uchikina."

"Kawai," came the whispered response. The man before him then pointed to the mat again.

Uchikina lay down, slowly becoming more comfortable with his partner. Kawai began to remove his customer's peasant disguise. Now, wearing only the *fundoshi*, Uchikina rested flat on the tatami.

The geisha moved a water basin to the side of the mat and began the ritual cleansing. Uchikina tried to relax as much as possible, but when the young fellow began undoing the last piece of clothing, his undergarment, it proved too much for him. *I am not ready for this!* No man had ever touched him in an intimate way before. Uchikina reached to dissuade the other from continuing.

From inside a hidden pocket, Kawai produced a red cord and began gently tethering Uchikina's hands and wrists together, palms facing, as if in greeting. From within its protective covering, Uchikina's erection pulsed harder with each brush of skin.

He could feel the sullied *fundoshi* being untied, but the cloth still lay beneath him on the tatami. The geisha resumed the bathing, this time swabbing Uchikina's private area. The cold water felt uncomfortable. When Kawai pulled back the loose skin of his penis and dabbed the cloth on the sensitive head, it felt like the push of a great river against a dam, wanting to burst forth and flow. Each swipe of the wet cloth brought him one step closer to finality.

Eventually the bath ended and Uchikina could relax a bit, knowing he was clean and ready for the pleasures to come. Kawai then removed a stalk of cherry blossoms from his hair and began stroking Uchikina's chest up and down, back and forth. When

Kawai leaned over and licked a nipple, cries of delight sprang from Uchikina's mouth. The young man smiled faintly at his accomplishment.

Next, Kawai sat atop Uchikina's waist and slipped his delicate legs under and around the calves of the customer. The gentle pressure of the intertwining limbs and the smooth stockings across his bare flesh added to the excitement, his prick leaking all the more.

Kawai stood, and seeing the dab of spunk shining at the tip of Uchikina's thick penis, he touched the fluid with his finger and then swabbed it across his protruding tongue. A grin of appreciation curved his mouth as Kawai continued to savor the taste of his client's juice.

The geisha then gently folded one of Uchikina's legs so that it bent at the hip and knee.

SLAP! he then heard.

"Hey!" cried Uchikina.

SLAP! was heard and felt again.

The boy kept smacking his client's delicate rump with an open palm.

SLAP! SLAP! SLAP!

This is supposed to be pleasurable, thought Uchikina, but then he realized his penis had thickened to the point of pain and the spunk at the tip of his cock leaked over and down. *Why is this so pleasurable? What is wrong with me?*

A ticklish feeling began to overshadow the sting of the slaps. Kawai had picked up the feather of a peafowl, long and wispy, and now swiped the delicate threads over Uchikina's reddened buttocks. The feather brushing continued up his chest, across his neck, down his side, between his thighs, and along the length of his taut manhood. An unbearable pressure built up inside Uchikina and he was about to discharge.

A tap on his erection, and the shaking of Kawai's head,

prevented the premature release of his pent-up sex. Kawai smiled with only half of his mouth, and Uchikina closed his eyes, ultimately giving up any control over the situation. With his hands tied, Uchikina could not touch his partner as his urges dictated. *I must do my part to satisfy. Please! Let me caress you.*

Uchikina flinched the first time Kawai fondled his testicles, but the skilled fellow continued giving pleasure to his assigned client. The graceful fingers traced the curves of the sack, the little wrinkles, playfully lifting and dropping each golden egg in turn. Uchikina's desire increased with each touch, though every time he felt the release approach, Kawai tapped the penis, training its master not to succumb too quickly.

After four or five close calls, the finger wandered down to Uchikina's hole, yet another place no one had ever touched before, not even his family physician. "Oh, oh," he cried as the geisha's dainty finger circled the crinkled opening. He could feel the wetness from his erection drip onto his lower abdomen. *How much longer can he tempt me? I must finish!*

Again the taps kept Uchikina from early completion, but now the finger began to poke through the band of muscle, wiggling as it penetrated. "*Mmm,*" hummed the satisfied customer. After a few minutes, Kawai had an entire exploratory finger inside the warm cavity, and more taps had to be administered.

Without warning, the finger abruptly withdrew. Uchikina opened his eyes to see Kawai stepping to the door, preparing to leave. *I hope this is no trick to catch me in disgrace and bring shame upon my family.* Even the doubting thoughts could not cause a reduction in the swelling at his midsection.

A few moments later, the geisha returned with a dish of shaved ice and a silver spoon. He closed the panel behind him and knelt next to Uchikina, offering a spoonful of frozen water. It refreshed the sweat-covered man instantly. He held his mouth open, begging for another scoop. Kawai dipped the spoon into the porcelain bowl and brought a mound of ice near to Uchikina's mouth, but would not let him eat it. The man strained his neck to reach the spoon, but the insolent young man kept moving it away. After an eternity of taunting, the cold ice fell into the waiting mouth.

Uchikina licked his lips and smiled at the satisfaction. Though, suddenly, he felt something very cold below. "Wait," blurted Uchikina as Kawai placed a scoop of ice on his penis. The sensation felt unusual, but as it was all part of the treatment, Uchikina simply allowed the practiced young fellow to continue his repertoire. Then again, what choice did he have?

Next, a warm mouth covered Uchikina's erection. It was almost too great a pleasure as a tongue teased the sensitive parts, plucking the cord, drumming the swollen head. Again, as the threshold approached, Kawai withdrew, but instead of taps, icy water from the bowl drizzled down his penis and onto his ball sack.

"Hey!" Uchikina howled. Kawai half-smiled again and continued alternating between warm and cold.

This is most pleasurable! I cannot believe I have waited so long to treat myself to such things. What an idiot I have been, mused the man dripping in his own juices.

Once again, Kawai used his mouth on Uchikina, but after a minute, he took the last bits of ice left in the bowl and inserted them quickly into the butthole of his writhing customer.

Uchikina spasmed and jerked, his eyes shut tight. *So much stimulation!* The warm in front contrasted with the freezing cold in the back. *So much torture! So much pleasure! How much more can I take?*

When Uchikina felt Kawai step away, he opened his eyes again. The geisha began to disrobe slowly and deliberately. Uchikina desperately wanted to stroke himself as he watched the beautiful young man reveal himself in ritualistic choreography.

Unfortunately, his hands were still tied, so that he could not reach the desired spot. However, his fat erection continued to pulse with delight at the visual stimulation.

First the *obi* came off, which was folded ceremoniously before being placed on a low table. Next, the silk kimono, with its intricate, flowery design of silver threads piercing the purple cloth, slid down from the shoulders and arms, revealing ivory skin beneath. Two pink, alluring circlets decorated the geisha's defined chest. Kawai then slipped off the red crepe woman's undergarment he wore instead of a *fundoshi*, and his large member thrust out like a curved sword. Lastly, he stepped off the *okobos*, losing a few inches of height. *What a vision!*

Once the geisha returned, he massaged Uchikina's penis with his tongue a few times to rekindle the heat. As the man on the mat once again neared climax, Kawai stopped the stimulation and spat profusely into his hands. Using the saliva as lubricant, he swabbed his own magnificent piece and placed the wide tip at Uchikina's tender hole.

No! No! thought Uchikina, unable to speak. But *yes, yes* was following close behind.

With his curious half smile, Kawai raised Uchikina's heels and plunged resolutely into the waiting abyss.

Waves of pain cut into Uchikina like a katana samurai attack. It hurt; it felt unbelievably good. He wanted it out; he wanted it never to leave.

Then the thrusting began. Over and over and over again, the geisha drove his piston in and out. Sweat began to pour down Kawai's painted forehead as he cultivated his own enjoyment. His long braids swayed as if a breeze blew through the cubicle, the strings of cherry blossoms swinging like the tails of agitated cats. The half grin became whole as the geisha sighed between thrusts.

The tempo of the pounding increased and slowed, increased

and slowed, for what seemed an hour. Both of them were sweating now, the mat growing damp beneath them.

Finally, Uchikina felt the skilled tongue of Kawai upon his engorged prick again. This time, nothing could hold him back, and a stream of hot come shot into the boy's voracious mouth before leaking down his delicate chin.

Kawai gave one last plunge, and Uchikina could feel a river pouring out of his crack, sticky and aromatic. The geisha grunted and groaned, then collapsed on top of him, heaving and sighing.

I wish I could hug him, but my hands are restrained, thought Uchikina. *This experience has been most delightful and I shall have to find a way to tip the boy, even though the practice is forbidden.*

The young man slowly moved off of Uchikina and knelt by his side, as if in prayer or meditation. After a few seconds of stillness, Kawai moved to retrieve the peahen feather and began to stroke it up and down his client's thighs, dancing it across his prick.

Oh, praise Buddha, there is more! Uchikina smiled. *I had no idea what exquisite services were to be provided.*

Once the stirring of the customer's shriveled cock began again, Kawai took it in his mouth and began to practice his oral skills. Within a minute, Uchikina was hard and dripping once more. As his restraints were still in place, he merely relaxed, trusting the geisha as he had never trusted anyone before.

Just as in the previous session, Kawai brought him to the brink a few times, tapping the customer's ready erection to prevent the shuddering end. After a few minutes of this blissful torture, the young man above spat profusely into his hands.

Oh no. Not again, Uchikina feared. *My tender parts still ache.*

He opened his mouth, about to object, but the practiced geisha put a saliva-laden finger to the man's lip to silence the protestation.

Uchikina realized, *I must trust that he will not hurt me.*

Again, the geisha produced profuse saliva into his hands, but this time he applied it to his client's stiff cock.

"*Mmm*," purred Uchikina.

Kawai positioned himself above the ready lance and slowly lowered himself down, until his tailbone rested upon Uchikina's hips.

"Aah," sighed Uchikina. *I have never penetrated another*, he mused. *So delightful!*

The boy began to swivel about, grinding his bottom on the man's steely tool and pressing his palms against the man's chest before twisting thick nipples between his slender fingers.

"Oh yes," moaned Uchikina.

And finally, the raising and lowering began. Slowly at first, allowing the client to nearly approach climax, but not permitting that pleasure too soon. Once the feeling subsided, the boy began the sweet torture again, varying speeds, up and down, up and down, the rhythm like a drumbeat.

"Yes, yes," groaned Uchikina, wishing the young fellow would just let him finish, yet realizing that the prolonging of pleasure was all part of the performance.

He glanced down and saw Kawai's massive prick bobbing around. It had been soft before, but now it had fully hardened and pointed toward Uchikina's face.

Soft squeals of delight escaped the boy's throat as he clawed at his client's chest and bounced off his hips faster and faster. Suddenly, streams of white juice slammed into Uchikina's nose, eyes, and mouth. The rhythmic contractions of Kawai's tight hole around his own cock propelled Uchikina over the brink, and he filled the young man's cavity with his molten flow.

Because his hands were tethered, Uchikina could do nothing to stop the burning sensation of his eyes and nose. However, the taste of his partner's thick spunk was a curious new delightful flavor.

Hmm, slightly salty, slightly sweet. He lapped his lips to retrieve every precious drop.

Kawai reached for a damp cloth and patted Uchikina's face to cleanse it. He then looked down into his customer's eyes as they both smiled simultaneously. The geisha spoke in a deep voice. "Thank you very much, Master."

Uchikina's eyebrows raised at hearing the feminine-looking fellow speak with such a man's tone. "Thank you, Kawai," he replied with a grin.

After a few more moments of exchanged smiles, the young man stood, dropped the cloth, grabbed his kimono and donned it. He motioned for Uchikina to stay put and then he left the cubicle once again.

Perhaps, I was wrong about this place, after all. Who knew what pleasures were to be found here? If only I could have had the courage to come to Yoshiwara sooner. If only I could have someone like Kawai at home. If only . . . Uchikina's thoughts rushed through his head.

The geisha returned with a basin of warm water and a few fresh cloths. He began bathing Uchikina ceremoniously before removing the red cord from the man's wrists. Once he completed the bath of his customer, he turned the attention to himself.

Uchikina started to stand, dressing himself in the disguise he had worn to conceal his true identity. He gazed down upon the man who had just brought him the supreme pleasures he had sought in coming to Yoshiwara. Kawai paused his cleansing briefly to look upward with fluttering eyes.

"Tomorrow?" Uchikina asked.

Kawai nodded in the affirmative. *Tomorrow . . .*

EIGHT NIGHTS

Richard May

A package was waiting for me Monday morning, wrapped in blue paper and white ribbon. The careful printing on the card attached read *Dear Steven, Happy Hanukkah*. I'm not Jewish but my name is Steven and it was my desk, so I untied the ribbon and pried apart the blue paper and gold tissue. Inside was a simple black rubber ring about two inches across. What kind of joke was this? A cock ring? Who would give me a cock ring? After staring at it awhile, though, I wondered if I should try it on. I stretched it tentatively between my fingers, but approaching voices made me quickly hide the thing.

Later, during a bathroom break, I slid it on in the privacy of a stall. My brain said, *Weird*, but my cock seemed to like it. It swelled, ready for action, so I let my right hand have its way with me. Afterward, I eased the thing off and went back to work—not that I accomplished much.

I pondered what kind of admirer would give me a cock ring. Images of cute Jewish men at the publishing company I worked for paraded through my thoughts. Still, when I made a tour and looked meaningfully at every guy there who I thought might be Jewish, no one looked meaningfully back.

The second day, another package said hello when I arrived. It was a little larger and softer than the first, but was also wrapped in blue and white, with a small card on top. *Happy Hanukkah* it repeated, adding *Wear me today*. I quickly opened and closed the tissue. It was a jockstrap—and it looked used. I waited five minutes and then thought, *Why not?*

Back in the same stall in the men's room, I held the jock up for a second look. It was white, or had been, and, yes, there were yellow stains on the crotch. Thinking about sharing cock space with another man made me horny. I rushed out of my slacks and boxers and slid the jock up my legs. The cup fit tight around my cock and balls. The straps bit into my ass. The waistband was just my size. *Hmm.*

That night, I introduced my first two gifts to each other. They played together nicely.

Wednesday, I arrived a half hour earlier than usual, but the package still beat me to my desk. This one was bigger yet, pliant but semihard—and, of course, so was I. I ripped into it. Inside was a black leather vest. Kinky. And expensive.

That night, in the privacy of my own ten-by-ten studio apartment (plus the kitchenette), I dressed up in all three presents and stared into my full-length mirror. Well, well. You *could* take the Midwest out of the boy. Suffice to say, I didn't get much sleep that night.

The fourth day, I left for work exceptionally early—I was up anyway, in more ways than one—and arrived around sevenish at my desk, which was bare. The rest of the morning, I hardly left my chair. I would catch this guy or burst my bladder, whichever happened first. Unfortunately, I had a lunch date with Scott in Accounting, my best friend at work.

At the deli we always went to, I told Scott about the Hanukkah presents.

"Wild," he said after swallowing a bite of brisket on rye. "Are you Jewish?"

"Do I look Jewish?"

"You can't always tell," he answered, staring at me over his sandwich. I had never noticed how tantalizing his eyes were or how aquamarine. They kept hold of mine while he chewed. I imagined him biting me—just a nibble here and there. Kinky, Steven. But Scott had never shown any interest in me.

"Well, anyway," I said, breaking the ocular connection, "I'm Presbyterian."

Scott looked amused, but, then again, he almost always did. He pushed back from the table. "Let's take a walk before we go back," he said and stood up, even though I hadn't finished my Coke. That was the only thing I didn't like about him; he had to decide everything.

Back at the office, there was a package on my desk, but it was just FedEx. Probably an author. Some of them still used print. Amy, my boss, came out of her office as I read the shipping label.

"Who's that from?"

"It doesn't say."

Amy clapped her hands in mock excitement. "Ooh! Mystery!"

I pulled the tear strip and peeked inside. A glimpse of blue wrapping paper paralyzed my hands.

"It looks like a present. Maybe it's for me," she said over my shoulder. Authors and agents sent her thank-you presents all the time.

"It was addressed to me," I muttered.

"Oh, well, what do you think it is? It's not your birthday, is it?"

"No, that's not until March."

I stalled, opening the FedEx packaging only incrementally, trying to think of an escape clause.

"Oh, let me do it," Amy huffed. She ripped the mailer out of my hands and the present out of the mailer. "Ooh, pretty paper. The card says *Happy Hanukkah*. *Use this*. Use this? What does that mean?" She folded her arms across her ample chest. "I didn't know you were Jewish."

I grabbed the present back. "I'm not."

"Well, *I am*. Maybe it's for me, after all," she said defiantly. Then I had to explain—without too many details—why it most likely wasn't. She started laughing, covering her mouth with her hands. "Stevie has an admirer. What else did he get you?"

"How do you know it's a he?"

"Duh," she answered, rolling brown eyes behind pink glasses. "Who do you think he is?" she asked.

"I went desk to desk," I lamented. "I couldn't tell. Maybe he doesn't work here."

Amy sighed deeply. "Steven, you have no gaydar."

She was probably right. In any case, I waited until she was back in her office and on the phone before I headed to the men's room. Stall number two was like my clubhouse now.

My fourth night present was an anal douche, chrome and very elegant looking. This douche said *I spent some money on you*. It also said *I want to stick something up your ass*. I rewrapped the package for later consideration. It would be my first time—for anal sex, at least.

That night, back home, I got naked, hooked the douche up in the shower, stuck the nozzle up my ass, and turned the faucet on. *Yow!* After a little heat adjustment, I filled 'er up and was ready to go. Not totally unenjoyable, by the way. Not at all.

Friday, I got to work at my usual time, clean through and through.

The fifth package was twelve inches long, slender, and hard. I had a bad feeling as I read the card. After *Happy Hanukkah*, it instructed me to *Practice after douching.* I removed the tape cautiously.

Damn! I had never seen one this big. I set it on my desk and it loomed even larger, leaning toward me, supported by two big balls. It was the lubricant enclosed that told me the dildo wasn't meant to be merely decorative. My ass hurt just thinking about it. I definitely needed some counseling.

"Scott Roth," a nonrecorded voice said after I punched his numbers into the phone.

"Oh, good. You're in already."

"Anything wrong, Steve?" he asked in his reassuring baritone.

"I'm not sure," I answered.

"*Okaaay.* Let's discuss it at lunch. See you in the reception area at twelve."

Good ol' Scott. Just what I needed: someone normal.

At lunch, he had his normal brisket sandwich and his normal iced tea. When I ordered an abnormal beer, he raised his eyebrows.

"I need alcohol," I explained.

"So, what's up?" he asked.

My head made a circuit of the crowded, noisy restaurant. I leaned in close. "I got a dildo today."

"The fifth night," he said meditatively, like everyone got a dildo on the fifth night of Hanukkah.

I leaned in closer. "Does it have a religious meaning?"

Scott's laughs were like barks rumbling up from his chest. Speaking of his chest, it was looking mighty good that day. Had he been working out? I also noticed his face was hairy.

"Are you growing a beard?" I asked.

"No," he said. "It's just the look." He shut up when the server arrived with our drinks. After she departed, he asked, "Are you afraid of it?"

"The beard? No, it looks great." He stared at me with those

stunning blue eyes. "Oh. The dildo," I said with a heavy sigh. Scott waited. "A little," I admitted, knocking back a lengthy slug of beer. "I mean, all of this is still pretty new to me." We considered my sexual inexperience momentarily.

"Did you use it?" Scott asked, after taking a sip of tea.

"Not yet," I said. He frowned. "I'm at work," I whined.

"*Hmm*," Scott said, like he was looking at photos. Our sandwiches appeared, and he stopped asking questions. I didn't blame him for not wanting any more lunch conversation about douches and dildos.

Once he finished, Scott paid and wouldn't take my money. "Keep it in your pants," he said, giving me a wink. Outside, we walked in tandem for a block, like we always did. We were about the same height and had equal strides.

"Maybe you won't get any more presents," he said, looking at me out of the corner of his eye.

"Aren't there three more nights?"

"It's the weekend," he said. He knew I never worked weekends. He observed me with his head tilted back. "Sounds like you want it. *Them*," he corrected himself.

"Maybe," I said vaguely.

Scott started us walking again while I ruminated. *Use dildo; don't use dildo. Use dildo; don't use dildo.*

Scott interrupted my musing. "Maybe you should just go with how you feel. Hey, speaking of which, do you feel like a movie tonight?" My little heart leapt. Scott hadn't suggested we get together outside of work before. On the other hand, there was the dildo and my instructions.

"I think I'm going to be busy tonight."

A strange light came on in his eyes. "You're going to use it, aren't you?"

I gulped. "I think so. But what about Saturday? I mean, for a movie," I said. I didn't want to lose my chance with him, just in case.

"Saturday's good," he said. "Let me look over what's playing, and I'll call you this afternoon." He steered us back into the office.

I sat at my desk, considering my date with Scott. Was it a date? I hoped so. Amy asked me why I was smiling. Who wouldn't be? I had two dates in one weekend, after all.

At home, I douched, turned up the radiator, donned my gay apparel, and lay on the sofa bed, ass on a towel, legs in the air. I lubed myself and the dildo so thoroughly I worried I wouldn't have enough to last the weekend.

I tentatively poked the beige head inside me. Did beige mean he was Caucasian? Sudden pain distracted me. Fuck! Was he this thick? And please don't tell me he was packing twelve inches! I thought about my mystery man's theoretical cock size while I eased the dildo along and, before I knew it, the dildo balls were smacking against flesh. Good job, Steve!

I began pushing and pulling. Pretty soon, I was saying *Fuck me, fuck me* like I was in a porn movie. My own cock ached, ready to explode, and then it did. A real gusher. I tried to imagine my Hanukkah Harry coming inside me, but I couldn't picture what he looked like.

Day six dawned. Even though it had been a late night with my dildo, I woke up early, like a kid at Christmas, wondering if I'd get anything. My aching asshole reminded me I'd gotten plenty. I played with myself a little, remembering. Someone buzzed to get in downstairs. Coitus interruptus. Probably crazy Charlene, locked out again.

"Charlene?" I asked the intercom.

"Yes," she said, giggling. It sounded like she had a cold.

I buzzed her in, but she kept buzzing back, so I put on my used jockstrap and a pair of baggy shorts and ran downstairs. No

Charlene, but there was a blue and white package in the foyer. HH had been here! I looked for him outside the vestibule, but saw no one likely, so I scooped up my latest present and double-timed back up the stairs.

The package was round and bumpy. That described what exactly?

The answer was a dog collar. Interesting. Let's review, Steven. Cock ring, jockstrap, vest, douche, dildo, dog collar. The card said *Be a good boy tonight.* Did he know I was going out? And, hey, how did he know my address? That was creepy—like, restraining order creepy.

I decided to make a latte. Coffee always helps me process.

The dog collar was human-sized. I ran my fingers along the pointy metal studs. "Why not?" I asked myself as I tried it on. The leather was cool and tight against my neck. I went to my mirror. *Woof!* "Okay, Steven," I then said out loud to myself, "let's do this." On went the cock ring, then the jock. I inserted my arms into the leather vest and looked in the mirror again. *Double woof, Dog Boy.* I considered douching and practicing with the dildo, but remembered I had a haircut appointment. Sex would have to wait.

At 5:45 I left again to take the subway south, meeting Scott at the station at 6:30 like he had told me to. He looked terrific, all in black, definitely more buff. How had I missed this development? We knuckle bumped. He liked my shorter hair.

"Keep it this way," he said, like it was a command, not a suggestion.

I followed him to a nearby theater. Afterward, I followed him to dinner. He didn't ask whether I had received another Hanukkah present. I waited until after he ordered our burgers before I told him.

"I got another Hanukkah present today," I said avidly. "A dog collar." The straight couple next to us suddenly looked interested, so I lowered my voice. "It was downstairs, in my building."

Scott whistled through his teeth. "Wow. How did he know the address?"

"Exactly."

"Did you put it on right away, in the foyer?" he asked, his voice a little husky.

How did he know there was a foyer? There's always a foyer, I told myself. "No, upstairs. In my apartment."

"When?"

Another odd question. "As soon as I got in the door."

He nodded and asked, "Did it fit?" What was this, an interview for the *Times*?

"Perfectly. Size sixteen."

Scott seemed to make a mental note, like he wanted to remember my shirt size for my birthday or something. Oh well, let him. Accounting made a lot more money than editorial.

"How did it feel?" he asked, his eyes narrowing.

I remembered how cool and tight the leather was around my neck, how hard and sharp the studs were against my fingers. "Good."

"Good?" he asked, clearly underwhelmed.

"Really good. Really hot," I said, leaning forward to whisper. That answer seemed more satisfactory. He pushed back from the table and grinned, resting his arms along the top of the booth. He was so cute. HH had told me to be good, but I began thinking very bad thoughts. Scott seemed to notice. He spread his legs.

"Why don't we take a walk?" I suggested nervously.

"I was thinking the same thing," Scott said, leering at me. "I live nearby. Just let me get the check."

"That's not what I meant!" I yelped.

Scott leaned in, still smiling, which was odd. "You don't want to?"

"No. I mean yes. I mean . . ." I didn't know what I meant. I shut up.

"Let's take that walk," he said, signaling for the bill.

We walked east. Scott lived somewhere nearby, I remembered. I had to think fast. Being good was about to be impossible. Then, I noticed we were outside a sex shop.

"Can we go in here?" I asked.

"Sure," Scott agreed, smirking. "What? Not getting enough toys from your mystery man?"

"I may need more lube."

Scott's smirk got even bigger.

Inside, I didn't know where to begin, but Scott pointed to the left. "Lube's over there." He was right. Lube, lube, lube, all kinds of lube. "This one's good," he said, handing me an enormous bottle. It was the same brand as my little one. "Sounds like you need the giant economy size." He gave me a wink. Thoughts of birds in bushes came to mind, but I resolved to take my lube and the number-six uptown.

We left the store and continued walking east. Soon, we were back at Astor Plaza. I stopped at the steps to the station.

"I live really close," Scott said, putting his hands on my hips and pulling me against him. He leaned in for a kiss, eyes closed. His lips were full. His body was hot. Our cocks were hard.

"No!" I shouted, startling several passersby.

Strangely, Scott didn't look disappointed. If anything, he seemed pleased. "Oh, right. You have to be a good boy. Another night maybe. If your mystery guy doesn't work out." He gave my butt a squeeze with both hands, which made me reconsider. Scott pushed me away though, laughing. "Come on, we'll get you a Lyft back to 78th Street. Somebody might mug you for the lube on the subway."

"That's funny," I said, chuckling. Then, a lightbulb went on. "Hey, how do you know where I live?"

He looked nonplussed for the first time in the seven months I'd known him, but quickly recovered his cool. "You told me," he answered.

"I did?"

"Yes, you did," he said firmly. He punched digits into his phone and announced, "Jason, the Lyft driver, will be here in five. I hope he's not cute."

While Jason—who was not cute—waited, Scott and I stared regrets at each other. He leaned in for a quick kiss, and I let him. There was no sustained contact and no tongue, so I figured it didn't count as bad behavior. Just two friends saying good night.

Scott shut the car door for me. As the car pulled away, he waved and gave me a lopsided grin, which was sexy as all hell. Suddenly, everything about Scott was sexy. Somebody would be a lucky dog tonight.

At home I showered, douched, and put everything on. I didn't even try to imagine the dildo wasn't Scott when I used it.

The next morning, my phone woke me, telling me it was almost ten. It was Scott, calling me on FaceTime.

"Hey," his voice said, all soft and breathy like he was lying next to me. He looked terrific.

"Hey back at you," I said, smoothing my hair.

"Don't worry," he said. "You look good all messed up." My heart did flip-flops. "So?" he asked, after a few moments of me staring lovingly at him on my iPhone.

"So?" I responded.

"What did you get?"

I jumped out of bed with the phone. "I don't know. I just woke up."

"Oh, dude, I'm sorry. I'll call back. By the way, you look great naked," he said.

I moved the phone back into head and shoulders territory and said, "Hang on. I'll go see if there's another present." I left Scott on the bed, facing the sheets, and got partially dressed. When I opened the door, I nearly tripped over the package. I carried it back to Scott, feeling for information along the way.

"It was right outside my door!" I said, showing him the present.

"Man!"

"I know."

"What is it?"

I put Scott faceup on the bed and tossed blue and white paper left and right. It was a dog leash. A dog leash! I showed it to him.

"Well, at least it coordinates with the collar."

"This is no joke, Scott."

"You're right; it isn't," he said solemnly. "Is this freaking you out too much? You know, you don't have to do anything. You're still in control."

"The thing is," I told him, "I'm not sure I want to be in control."

"Really?" Scott said. His face had a look I'd never seen before. *Feral* was the word that came to mind.

"I don't know," I answered. My voice quavered. "It's a dog leash."

Scott's face relaxed. He repeated that I didn't have to do anything with it or about it.

"I know some guys who would," I said, trying to make a joke.

"So do I," Scott agreed seriously.

A *non sequitur* from him changed the subject. "Your dog's a golden retriever, right?" he asked.

"How did you know?"

He gave me a look. "The photo on your desk?"

It was of my parents, as well as my family's dog. "Right," I said, wondering where we were going with this.

"What's his name?"

"Boy," I replied.

"Boy?" Scott asked, looking incredulous.

I hated telling this story. "Boy the Second, really. When we got Boy the First, my dad said, 'Here boy,' so I thought that was the puppy's name." Scott laughed. Such a nice laugh, rumbling up from his chest. Such a nice chest. Damn! Why hadn't I said yes last night?

"Want to meet for brunch?" he asked in the middle of my self-recrimination.

"Sure!" I agreed enthusiastically before I could ask myself whether a second date with Scott constituted being good. "Where shall we meet?"

"I'll come to you," Scott answered. "What's the address?"

"You mean you don't remember?"

"Huh?"

"I told you, right?"

He laughed a little weirdly. "Right."

At noon, I buzzed him in and waited on the landing. "You're almost there," I yelled down to him when I saw his dark, wavy hair come into view. He looked up, grinning and looking better than a body has a right to. When he reached my landing and stood next to me, he seemed taller than usual.

"You grew," I said.

"Boots," he replied. I looked at his feet. Big clod-stomping boots, my grandfather would say. On their way down Scott's body, my eyes noticed how good his leather jacket looked on him and how enticing the bulge at his crotch was. I lingered along his meaty thighs and calves, which were so much more noticeable in tight jeans than his standard work slacks.

I made my eyes return directly to Scott's face, with no further stops along the way. He looked around, a smile on his face. We were still in the hall. "I'm sorry!" I said. "Come in; I'll show you my toys."

I deposited everything on the sofa bed. Scott examined each gift like he was examining me. "We better go," I said quickly, standing up.

Scott looked at the bulge in *my* crotch. "I'd sure like to see you in all this," he said in a voice like a growl.

"Scott . . ."

"Okay, okay. I know. Help me up." He reached an arm up, and I pulled him to his feet. "You sure?" he asked, holding on to my shoulders, brushing his erection back and forth over mine. I wasn't, but I broke his hold anyway.

"Let's eat," I said in a very shaky voice.

And so eat we did. And stared into each other's eyes. Still, I was a good boy—until later that evening when I played with myself and my toys for hours. My Hanukkah Harry had a face now, at least in my mind's eye—and a body. It was Scott's face looming over me, and his cock pumping my ass. I had to take two pills to get to sleep, which meant I woke up late on Monday morning. I sent Amy a text apologizing. She sent back an *!* and a *?*, as I was never late. When I finally rushed into the office, everyone stopped what they were doing and watched me approach my desk.

I couldn't believe it. My desk was empty except for a teensy little card. Wasn't this supposed to be the big one? I ignored everyone and tore open the envelope. The card still read *Happy Hanukkah* on the front. Yeah, yeah. The message inside was: *You remind me of your dog. Same hair color. Come to this address tonight at 6 o'clock to get your final Hanukkah present. Wear everything. Bring the leash. Don't forget to douche.*

Hanukkah Harry was certainly bossy.

I called Scott and he met me downstairs for coffee. I showed him the card.

"My neighborhood," he said. "Are you going?" One thick eyebrow arched.

"I don't know."

"After all this? Don't you want to know who he is?" He sounded exasperated.

I shrugged. "I'm sort of interested in someone else now."

"Do I know this someone else?" He sounded jealous. That made me feel all warm inside.

"Yes."

"And you're not going to tell me who he is?"

"Absolutely not."

He thought a moment. "You should go," he said in that irritatingly decisive way he had, but I agreed with him. I wanted to know who the guy was, and this might be my only chance. After all, Hanukkah was over at sundown.

"Want to have lunch today?" Scott asked.

"No," I told him. "I have an errand to run."

I left work early and rode an Uber home with my purchase. I douched extra, extra carefully and took a long shower. Once I was clean inside and out, I put on the cock ring, dirty jock, and the vest. I stepped into ripped jeans and threaded a wide black leather belt through its loops. I pulled on my new engineer boots—I'd bought them at lunch, inspired by Scott's pair—clicked the dog collar into place around my neck, and slipped my arms into a leather jacket. I stared at myself in the mirror. What the hell was I doing? I collapsed onto the sofa bed and called Scott.

"What do you mean you're not going?" he yelled into the phone.

"This guy could be crazy!"

He spoke more calmly. "You're right. Well, then, why not meet me for dinner at Little Kiev? I'd like to see you in all your Hanukkah presents."

A third date! Without a second thought, I said, "Okay!"

After another trip downtown, I saw a man waiting outside the restaurant. He was about my height, dressed in a black leather harness, skintight leather pants, and engineer boots. Slender but well muscled. Except for the harness, his torso was bare. He wore a biker's cap and dark sunglasses. His skin was pale, pale olive. He was Scott.

"Wow!" I said. "You look great!"

"So do you," he answered, turning me around.

After dinner, he announced, "I have a Hanukkah present for you back at my place." I didn't need any more gifts and certainly didn't need any additional motivation to go home with him. In fact, I had an erection all through our kielbasa combos.

After he shut the door to his apartment and set the deadbolt, Scott again looked me up and down. "What about your secret admirer?" he asked tentatively. I shrugged. He seemed to like that response. "Did you bring the leash?" he asked, suddenly stern, causing my body to tremble.

"No," I answered uncertainly. He removed my jacket and hung it up.

"What about the dildo?"

I shook my head. He looked disappointed.

"Next time," he said. *Next time!* I thought happily. "Do you want your present now?" he asked. Without waiting for an answer, he pulled me into his bedroom. "Strip," he said. "Except for the jock."

"Yes, Sir," I barked. I could play the game, if that's what he wanted. In fact, I'd been aching to play this game with him, not Hanukkah Harry. When I finished, Scott traced the erection inside my jock and felt for the cock ring.

I had it on and— "Stay," he said abruptly, showing the carpet the flat of his hand. He retrieved another blue and white package, which I opened carefully, wondering whether it was a new shirt. It wasn't. Scott's Hanukkah gift to me was a mask—a dog mask.

"Are you sure about this?" I said.

He nodded. "Put it on."

Somewhat reluctantly, I slipped the mask over my head. I worried I wouldn't be able to see or breathe, but, to my relief, the eyeholes were large and the snout had holes for air. I took my first breath inside the mask.

Scott checked it for fit and my comfort. When satisfied all was well, he told me to get down on all fours. "You douched, right?" he asked, with some enticing menace to his voice. I started to answer, but he interrupted. "You're a dog," he reminded me, so I barked twice for yes. Scott stroked my back. "Good boy," he cooed before he started to stick a hard, cold object up my ass.

I yelped several times in surprise. It was as big or bigger than the one Harry had sent me.

"Relax," Scott commanded and eased the dildo all the way in. "You've been practicing," he said, and pulled it out. "You're clean," he said. "Good boy," he repeated, patting my head. Behind me, I heard him unzip his leather pants. He then slid them down his thighs, tore open a package, and put a condom on. I yelped again when his fingers inserted cold lube inside me, but it still felt amazing to have even a little bit of Scott inside me.

"Quiet!" he said sharply, jerking my head back by my hair. I obediently tried not to make another sound. "Yes," he groaned as he pushed inside me, grunting each time he slammed against my ass. He kept telling me what a good dog I was.

"Happy Hanukkah," he whispered, licking my ear and reaching for my cock. We barked in unison as we came.

"Happy Hanukkah," I repeated, panting. It had taken twenty-two years and eight nights, but I had my miracle—and it was a big one.

REFLECTIONS

Michael Roberts

"Don't touch that butt," he said.

I presumed that Dr. Anderson meant the butt of his young pulchritudinous assistant, who was perched on a ladder reaching for a book on a shelf above our heads. One foot was a step higher than the other, and his lightweight trousers stretched over a well-formed tush and thigh and no underwear line, presenting an extremely tempting target. Chauncey, the assistant, looked over his shoulder at me, a winsome smile on his enchantingly handsome face.

I could understand why he and the scientist both seemed to think that my floating finger was reaching for a friendly little pinch of his bottom. I have something of a reputation, probably deserved, for putting my hands in unexpected places. Nothing ventured, nothing gained is my motto. Sometimes I gain a slap or a dislocated jaw, but they seem a small price to pay for the much more pleasurable rewards I've accrued.

I presumed that Dr. Anderson had been a bit peremptory with me because he had a proprietary interest in the posterior that he thought I was approaching. That sounds a great deal worse than it was, because whatever the relationship between Dr. Anderson—Quentin—and Chauncey, it was mutual. And it wasn't as if Quentin were a dirty old man. Yes, he was somewhat lascivious, and he was of a different generation, but since gay generations are unlike straight generations, that merely meant that Quentin was in his thirties and Chauncey was in his twenties, and I was somewhere in that age range.

And yes, we were in Quentin's laboratory, where there were all sorts of containers and control panels and gadgets, so I probably should have known better than to lay a hand on anything or anyone. But above this button was a little sign that read DANGER, and I hadn't ever seen a sign like that before in the lab, and it stirred my curiosity, and one of my failings is, as I've already indicated, the fact that I can't resist fulfilling my curiosity.

Anyway, by the time I understood that Quentin meant to say, "Don't touch that button," and not, "Don't touch that butt," my darting digit had already alighted on my objective and pressed the button, not Chauncey. Half a second later, there were two whoops of a high-pitched alarm and we were in total darkness, and Dr. Anderson said, "Shit."

"I didn't realize that's a light switch," I told them regretfully.

"It isn't," responded Quentin, and in the darkness, I couldn't be sure, but it sounded as if he was speaking through teeth tightly clenched.

"But it turned off the lights," I said, reasonably enough, I thought.

"Yes, Martin, you dunderhead, it did." He seldom called me *dunderhead*, so I presumed that he was very annoyed with me. "But it's not—oh, you won't believe me."

"We can't know until you try."

"No," he said, "I guess we can't," and he took, audibly, a deep breath. "I haven't told you that I've been working on some experiments."

"Oh, have you really?" I asked, raising my eyebrows and grinning widely at him, but of course he didn't know that, since the lights were off.

"Not that kind of experiment, you twit," he snapped.

Dunderhead and *twit* in the space of a few minutes. My, I had aroused the Anderson ire.

A brilliant bolt zapped through the darkness. Quentin said, "Shit!" again, and there was a sizzle, and the lights crackled back on.

I couldn't see that I'd done any damage. Nothing had been destroyed or even harmed. No one had been hurt. There was Quentin standing where I'd last seen him, and there was the delightful Chauncey on the ladder, and there was Chauncey at one of the control panels, and there was Chauncey at a table pouring bubbling liquid into a beaker, and something was not right.

I waved wordlessly at the three Chaunceys, and Quentin said, "Yes, you dunderheaded twit."

To which I replied, "What happened?"

"What happened," replied Quentin, and the timbre of his voice was about three notes higher than usual, "is that you've spoiled my experiment. I've been working on cloning human beings, and I was using Chauncey as my model, and I had a few more adjustments to make, but you had to yet again put your finger where it doesn't belong and gum up the works."

"I'm sorry—" I began.

"You're always sorry, Martin, but your apologies and regrets are, as usual, too little, too late."

I drew myself up and said, in what I hoped was a regally haughty tone, "Well, Quentin, now I know what you really think of me."

"Oh, don't do your 'poor misunderstood Martin' routine. It won't work this time."

At that moment, Chauncey—I mean, another Chauncey—walked in from an adjoining room, and I squeaked, "How many of them are there?"

"I don't know," moaned Quentin. "I hadn't concluded the research, and I hadn't set a number, and for all I know, there are Chaunceys in every room in this building, in every building on this block, on every street in this city—ohhh," he concluded, and held his head.

"Well," I said, "that can't be completely bad. As we both know, Chauncey is an exquisite specimen of youthful manhood, and several of him roaming about are surely going to improve the landscape."

Chauncey smiled at me, and Chauncey smiled at me, and Chauncey smiled at me, and Chauncey smiled at me.

"I don't know if all of the quality controls worked," continued Quentin in a low voice, sounding somewhat like the opening of a Mahler symphony.

"They look all right to me," I said, and regarded each Chauncey in turn, flawless reflections of each other, epitomes of beauty. Each Chauncey tilted his head and opened wide his mouth in an expansive grin, and the dazzle from the perfect sets of teeth blended into a luminescence that was absolutely blinding.

Then the Chauncey at the control panel looked at the Chauncey on the ladder, and a sly smile spread over his charming countenance, and he said, "I think that we've developed okay, don't you?"

And Chauncey returned to the shelf the book he held in his hand, and he said, "Oh, I think so, too."

"Shall we show them?" asked the other Chauncey.

"We shall show them," said the ladder Chauncey.

He turned so that his back was against the ladder, and balancing with one hand on a rung, he removed his shoes and tossed them onto the floor, and he unzipped his pants and let them fall—and indeed he wasn't wearing shorts—and he lifted first one leg and then the other and shook the trousers onto the floor beside the shoes, and his cock, his long slender cock, bounced out from the tail of his shirt.

Quentin perhaps was familiar with the sight of Chauncey's inspirational prick, but I wasn't, and I was rendered quite speechless, quite immobile—well, not entirely immobile. By the time I'd somewhat recovered from the spectacle of such sweet masculinity unfettered and had checked the panel Chauncey, his legs too were bare, and his cock, his long slender cock, was pointing toward me in a most alluring fashion. The third Chauncey had abandoned his beaker and his trousers and was extending quite nicely from the bottom of his shirt. And the last Chauncey, the last that we knew about at least, was standing in the middle of the room, pantsless, like a really entrancing blossom.

The four Chaunceys looked at each other, and the ladder lad, the beaker boy, and the middle-of-the room rendition went to stand by the panel Chauncey, and in precise synchronization they unbuttoned their shirts and let them waft to the floor like flags of mad abandon and then stood in artful array before Quentin and me, with their hairless swimmer's chests, their neat little triangles of pubic hair, their pleasingly firm pricks pointing at us.

I glanced at Quentin to see if he was as moved by this sensual vision as I was, but he was staring at the Chaunceys à quatre so intensely that his glasses were misting over.

After the four Chaunceys had basked in the adoration that they had inspired in Quentin and me, the Chauncey on the far left looked at the Chauncey on the far right, and the two Chaunceys in the middle looked at each other, and all of them nodded. Then the two left Chaunceys looked at each other, and the two right Chaunceys looked at each other, and they nodded. It was like being in a hall of mirrors, watching eyes move simultaneously, heads bob in concert, gorgeous men breathe in concupiscent chorus. And as if all had thus agreed that the middle Chaunceys would sort of ripple over to Quentin and me, they did, while the remaining two Chaunceys stared at us with affable smiles that were a bit tinged with mischievousness.

One Chauncey stood in front of me, and one Chauncey stood in front of Quentin. I think it was at that moment that I began to perspire, because it certainly isn't every day, or every other day, for that matter, or any day besides this continually amazing day, actually, that I gaze into the eyes of a ravishing young man without a stitch on and can see past his shoulder the backside of a ravishing young man without a stitch on and past him the features of my friend, who, apparently, is trying to decide whether to fall onto the floor in a swoon.

Then, as if at some invisible, inaudible sign, the Chaunceys each stretched out a hand and gently lowered Quentin and me to the floor. At that point, of course, I completely forgot about the doctor and his companion, because staring me in the face was the faultless flower of my Chauncey's manhood. (I considered him my Chauncey because the appeal, the allure was so overpowering that I felt as if his prick were a wand that he had waved before me and cast a spell that made only him and me exist.) Oh, that manhood was long and slender, as I may have said, and exquisitely toned and proportioned, and behind and below were two impeccably shaped balls that were like extra sacks of sweets behind that tempting stick of candy extending toward me.

He grinned down at me and moved his stunning sex into my mouth, which was open with amazement and admiration. Out of the corner of my eye, just before my peripheral vision was consumed by the lushness of his bush, I saw the second Chauncey move at the same moment toward Quentin and presumably go between Quentin's lips.

And then I forgot about Quentin and his Chauncey because the taste of this young man's member was moist and delicate and strong and exhilarating and just, well, absolutely scrumptious. He slid it in and out, and I glanced up at his face, and he was smiling like an angel in a Renaissance painting.

Yes, he was divine in face and body, and the flavor of his cock was rich and rare. I have savored enough cocks in my lifetime—well, never enough cocks, of course; can there ever be enough cocks?—and this cock was unlike any other I've had the pleasure of experiencing.

I cupped his rousingly rounded buttocks in my hands, and it was as if I were touching an amalgam of the firmest alabaster and the supplest of clouds. He tilted back his head, and he closed his eyes, and a drop of the most delicate distillation fell onto my tongue, and I was as inebriated as if I had drunk an entire bottle of the bubbly.

More of this intoxicant followed, and my head was spinning, and there was a rushing in my ears as if I were in the midst of a mighty wind.

Just as I felt I was going to topple in this tempest, there was a covey of butterflies at my butt, and this covey seemed oddly intent on removing my pants. When I heard a giggle at my end, and thought that I heard a concurrent chuckle a few feet away, I realized that the third Chauncey was parked at my aft and the fourth Chauncey was probably installed at Quentin's backside, and the butterflies had been the fluttering fingers of the third Chauncey undoing my belt and slipping down my trousers while the fourth Chauncey was disrobing Quentin.

I lifted my lower half to help this process, which no doubt put me at one of my less flattering angles, and off went my slacks and off went my underwear. In a bit of a chill, I returned my knees to the floor and continued to relish Chauncey's delectable dick.

Eagerly, I waited to see what would happen next.

What happened next was the snap—no, the double snap of what I was reasonably sure, or as reasonable as I could be under the circumstances, of two condoms. This entire episode was like a dream, and I expected to wake at any moment and find wet spots all over me and the bed that were entirely mine, the Chaunceys disappearing in my unwelcome return to consciousness. But I didn't wake, and so I became sure, absolutely sure, well, reasonably sure, that I felt a Chauncey cock touching delicately the crest of my nether regions, tracing down the division, top to bottom, then up, then down, then pressing between the halves, pressing as far as it could go without intruding, and withdrawing, and pressing, as if it were shyly slyly asking if its presence were welcome. Its presence was decidedly definitely welcome, but I couldn't split the quivering silence to say so. Evidently, that wandering cock knew that my silence was assent, because after a few more passes up and down and up and down my ass, it entered.

My breath was taken away; for a moment, inhalation, exhalation stopped, and I reveled in the subtle stab of Chauncey's cock, firm yet graceful, compelling yet tactful, no overbearing thrust, but no weakness, either. It seemed as if Chauncey's cock was the cock for which I had been waiting a long time and that wondrously brought magic to my asshole.

What a fantastic feeling of completeness the Chaunceys granted me, one of them in my mouth and one in my rear end, a condition I wished to prolong as much as possible.

But how much time *would* be possible? Chauncey's marvelous dick was getting harder and harder in my mouth, and it was dispensing more and more flavorsome fluids, and his sighs were increasing in volume and intensity. If I thought about it, I could hear a sort of echo as if Quentin's Chauncey was percolating with the same ardor, but I didn't think about it much, because I was so spellbound at my Chauncey's profuse prick between my greedy, grasping lips as well as the compelling cock gliding down and over and through my rearward roadway.

And then Chauncey said, quite ringingly, "Oh!" And because it was so ringing, I suspected that the Chauncey inserting his adorable appendage into Quentin's mouth had also said, "Oh," ringingly, and their voices rang ensemble. And although I'd like to attribute my Chauncey's copious coming to my fellating skills, which I've been told are considerable, I can't in honesty do that, since Quentin's Chauncey peaked at the exact same time. So maybe Quentin and I, laboring together, produced a concomitant climax from both Chaunceys, who were bound together by virtue of their being—well—Chauncey.

Chauncey put a silky hand on my cheek—the facial one—and smiled and trailed his fingers through the little lake of jism that overflowed the corners of my mouth, and he withdrew. He withdrew, presumably, at the particle of a second at which his compatriot withdrew, because I was suddenly face-to-face with Quentin, both of us on our knees, both of us dribbling down one side of the jaw, with the third and fourth Chaunceys behind us, seesawing in and out, in and out, splendidly in and out.

Quentin was wearing his glasses, although, given the amount of humidity that had condensed thereon, he probably couldn't see a thing. I could see the wavering double of myself in the lenses, and behind me, diving and driving into me, Chauncey, in the fluctuating fucking reproduction just like a beacon of light, an otherworldly being whose cock did not feel otherworldly, whose cock felt magnificently substantial and soothing.

I glanced above Quentin, and his Chauncey was staring at my

Chauncey, who was presumably staring back. I might have felt some resentment that they were so wrapped up in each other and not the men in whom their cocks were so wrapped up, but considering the pleasure I was achieving from the barrage of dickly delight upon my ass, I decided to be the better man and forego my annoyance.

Chauncey was playing me like a musical instrument, his prick a bow that was producing pitches and tones and melodies that I had not known were within me, that burst forth while Chauncey was within me. I saw myself in the steam of Quentin's glasses, and even in that distortion, I could see the pleasure on my face. It was an interesting experience, since I hadn't watched myself being fucked before, at least from that angle. It was like being in a porno movie and watching the movie at the same time, especially looking back and forth between my elated visage and Chauncey fucking Quentin and thence to Chauncey fucking me. Then Chauncey executed a particularly nice anal maneuver, and I felt my eyes roll up in my head, which meant that I couldn't see anything anymore except a sort of palpitating brightness.

The volume was increasing as the Chaunceys cried out in tandem, as I could hear myself panting, as I could hear Quentin—well—barking, accompanied by the slip-slap of flesh on flesh, Chauncey's balls smacking against my buttocks, Chauncey's balls hitting Quentin's ass.

I was assaulting myself vigorously with one hand, trying to support myself with the other hand. My stomach was racing around within me as Chauncey's cock was racing within me, and I would have been quite happy if these hyperbolic circumstances could have continued indefinitely, say maybe for the next five or six years. However, it was becoming increasingly obvious that the circumstances were getting quite definite, because it was becoming more and more difficult to keep myself on the brink of orgasm rather than crashing over it. Quentin was turning mauve, and his Chauncey threw back his head, and probably my Chauncey did, too. There was then an ululation in stereo as the Chaunceys pushed Quentin and me to the floor and vociferously came, voluminously came, and I stickily surged all over myself and the floor, and someone was yelling, and it was probably me.

I have no idea how much later I returned to consciousness—somewhat—and I was still lying on the floor. I opened my eyes and stared into Quentin's face, on which his glasses hung lopsidedly, and he stared nearsightedly back at me, and we regarded each other like amoebas that have landed on a strange and baffling beach.

I have no idea how much later I gained coherence—a little—and remembered the remarkable set of circumstances that had brought me to this prone position on the floor of Dr. Anderson's laboratory.

I unglued myself from the floor and unsteadily arose and looked around, hoping to see again the striking young men who had conveyed me to my aching condition, but I didn't see them. There was a small puddle behind me, and as Quentin stumbled upward, I saw that there was a puddle behind him, and there was one a few feet away from the site of our tussle with the Chaunceys. Of course, a lot of the puddling on the floor was Quentin's and mine, but these particular puddles, I thought, were not.

Nonplussed, Quentin and I gazed at each other. It is disconcerting to be naked and view the body of your friend, also naked, who is, of course, viewing you right back, and both of you, shall we say, in an untidy shape, and neither one has seen his friend in such a condition resulting from actions that you assumed he committed but had never seen him commit, hadn't intended to see him commit. Anyway, there's now a whole new spin to the friendship.

So, we looked away and around and saw Chauncey on the ladder by the shelves reaching for a book. And he seemed to sense our eyes on him, for he turned and beamed at us.

"Chauncey," said Quentin, and his voice cracked and he had to begin again. "Chauncey, where are your friends?"

"My friends?" responded Chauncey.

"Your friends. Well, I mean the images of you, your doubles, your triples, your—the others."

"The others?" responded Chauncey, and his face was the absolute illustration of innocence. "I'm afraid, Dr. Anderson, that I don't know what, or whom, you're talking about."

Quentin coughed loudly and lengthily and said, "Well, the lights went off after Martin pressed, yet again, the wrong thing"— he aimed a barbed look at me—"and then they came back on."

"Yes," said Chauncey, "and you and Martin were . . ." He looked, in seeming discomfort, at the floor. "You and Martin were—*you know*."

"No," said Quentin and I together, "we don't know."

"You were—ah—*with each other*, and I didn't think that it was my place to . . . and so I didn't; I just let you two do what you were doing with each other."

For a moment, Quentin and I were speechless—which I seldom am.

Then he said, "Do you suppose?" He gestured to him and me, and I said, "No. Certainly not."

Then he said, "Do you suppose?" He made a sort of encompassing sweep with his hand, and I said, "Yes. Well, I suppose."

Then he said, "Do you suppose?" and indicated the puddles on the floor. "Or," he added, and pointed at the exit door, and I said, "Yes, it's entirely possible. Although—"

And then we both looked at Chauncey, the one and only Chauncey—maybe—and I might have believed his ingenuous smile, but there was a twinkle in his eyes, which could have been a trick of the lights, and I imagined that I saw in that twinkle the shining reflection of Chauncey—and Chauncey—leading me to sexual satisfaction, and I grinned back at Chauncey, and thought that no matter what had happened, it was one of the most fabulous afternoons I'd ever spent.

LEGEND

Dale Chase

I never paid much attention to the house at the top of the hill until police and paramedics appeared. The officer who chased me off acted like my approach was a breach of national security, as if a pool man could pose any sort of threat. I retreated reluctantly, huffing at the injustice, since I wouldn't get paid for work not done.

Sitting in my truck, I watched cops move in and out. I counted nearly a year of work behind those gates, sweeping the pool in absolute silence. Not once had anyone appeared; not once had I glimpsed anything more than a squawking scrub jay or dragonfly buzzing the water. I'd long ago written off the occupant as elderly, someone unwilling or unable to muster curiosity, because I couldn't begin to consider that anyone in his prime might ignore my presence—especially since I provided sexual services to my customers down the hill.

I loved the life, lived the cliché to the fullest, fucking aging moguls, up-and-coming hotshot producers, oftentimes sucking cock before I got anywhere near the pool. My salary was modest; tips for the extra services were not.

The topmost house had always looked tired, an aging, two-story Spanish style with stucco fallen away in places and fissures along staircases. The garden was more rampant than lush, overgrown with a generous mix of orange and lemon that gave everything a citrusy smell. The lawns were mowed but the rest of it looked heavy, in need of pruning, and I wondered why they paid a pool man but not a decent gardener. Was the owner a swimmer who darted out to the water and rushed back inside, never noticing his shrubbery gone mad?

In any case, the following week all returned to normal, except I worked with new curiosity. I asked my boss about the place, and he told me he didn't know who lived there, that an accounting firm paid the bills. Now, as I pushed my brush along the pool sides, I felt eyes on me for the first time. In response, I stripped away my shirt, then slowed everything down, easing the pole into the water, pushing and pulling with long, languid strokes. Periodically, I paused to wipe my brow and look around, twice stopping altogether to drink some bottled water. The second time I did this, a man stepped out onto the patio. I knew instantly who he was.

Thinner than I recalled, and absent the usual tan, he still maintained an almost regal presence, as if there were no bandages on his wrists. His once golden hair had gone platinum, still full but now uncombed, shaggy at the ears. He wore white slacks, an untucked white shirt, no shoes.

We said nothing, even though I'd stopped work, and I watched him draw his hands to his chest and clasp them together. His expression remained blank, but he still exuded an incredible power, as if he could draw the world itself to him. I began to understand the force that had made him the star he'd once been.

I moved to him as I knew countless others had. I understood them now, willing captives eager to do whatever he asked. And for once I wasn't propelled by the urgency I found at houses down the hill. This was different, a unique kind of beckoning, everyday lust elevated to a higher plane. As I neared him, my life gradually came into focus, how I'd been living. Fucking. Nothing more. Suddenly, things were changing—in all of forty feet.

When I reached him, he didn't smile. There was no welcome beyond a single finger drawn not down, as expected, but up, along my jaw and cheek.

His eyes were pale blue, his features, once matinee-idol sharp, now almost too pronounced, gauntness added to the mix. He was still handsome in his diminished state, but shrouded in sadness. *It's Leland Cady*, I reminded myself, *screen legend*.

He didn't lead me inside; he simply turned and let me follow. I found the house an elegant chaos, neglected, dusty. A broken lamp lay on the floor. He stepped around it as if it were nothing more than an ottoman or potted plant.

He led me upstairs to what I could tell was not his bedroom. Bare and musty, it was unoccupied except for the bed, where the covers were so tangled I knew it had not been a good night for its occupant. This got me to wondering what had driven him from his own space. The scene I crafted in my head made him all the more tragic and, therefore, all the more appealing.

I undressed him slowly, revealing a timeworn but still beautiful body, a dusting of platinum hair across his chest, a stripe of it descending to the silky bush at his beckoning crotch.

He wasn't aroused, which initially surprised me, since my other customers often met me at the door sporting erections. I quickly stripped away my jeans and boots, watching him watch me. He eyed my swollen prick with an almost resigned hunger, as if even the idea of sustenance exhausted him.

I outweighed him by a good twenty pounds and stood about four inches taller, something I could tell he liked. I knew instinctively he wanted someone strong, that he needed things done to him. I slid a hand around my cock and gave it a stroke, while he let out a whimper and began to cry.

I didn't go to him. Instead, I let his tears flow, all the while working myself. His hands hung at his sides, his cock still limp, but I knew this was what he needed, that his sadness and pain were ultimately caught up in his most basic need.

He didn't wipe away his tears, and when he kneeled, he went down shakily, as if life had weakened him. He rubbed his face against me and I let go of my prick. His tongue did all the work at first, which underscored his hunger. He licked my dark pubes and the base of my cock, then drew along its length and played at the head, never taking hold but still feeding, as if he could lick down through the layers of flesh to get to the come.

I did nothing. As much as I wanted to grab him and shove my dick down his throat, I wanted more to soothe, so I let him do what he needed. When he finally took me fully into his mouth, he looked up as if for reassurance. It was then that I knew he wanted to submerge and never come up for air.

Of course, he was expert. Shudders ran back through my ass as he delicately pulled and sucked, as his tongue played with my crown. And when he released me and went under to my bag, I broke the silence, offering a long moan as he got one, then both of my balls into his mouth. It was all I could do not to grab myself and finish.

I let him feed for some time, but finally there was no choice. I eased him up to find the bed, where he rolled onto his stomach, then stuck his rump up at me. As I stared at the sight and told myself I was about to fuck the great Leland Cady, he reached back, pulled open his cheeks, and flexed his muscle. "Oh, man," I said as I quickly retrieved a rubber from my pants pocket, lubed my dick with spit, and climbed on.

I went in easily, then felt him clamp down and hold on, compensating, most likely, for a well-traveled path. It didn't matter to me; I was in.

When I began to ride him, he began a near-primal wail that kept up throughout. I hung on to his hips, noted how narrow they were, how white, and I listened to the juicy slap of flesh and my own rhythmic grunt. It was like an orchestra, fuck-sounds beating a literal cadence.

I wanted to last but wasn't going to. He needed hours of this—I could tell from the way he took it, the way he sounded—but once my load began to rise, none of that mattered. I flattened myself onto him, wrapped my arms around his chest, and pumped his ass until I began to erupt. He in turn began to squeal. I knew he was coming, that taking dick had gotten him hard and set him off on his own fuck-journey. I pounded him until I was empty, until my spent cock slid out. He immediately curled onto his side away from me while I, after discarding the condom, was at a loss as to what to do next.

I noticed he was still tense, shoulders hunched, head down. I'd never seen this before. Sex always undid people, but here was one who it wound even tighter. I slid an arm around him as tentatively as possible, ready to retreat at the first sign of resistance, but he eased back against me and I knew he needed more than cock— consolation, possibly, company at the very least.

He lay so still that I thought at first he'd gone to sleep, but then he moved just the slightest, as if he knew my thoughts and wanted me to know an approach was welcome. I reached around and took his wrist in hand. "What happened?" I asked.

"Jeffrey happened," he said. "I fell in love with my gardener. Two years of hell, but, of course, I'd do it all again, would welcome him in an instant, hand him the fucking knife."

I nuzzled his neck before he continued. "I have a thing for earth boys, you see, beautiful young creatures who cut nature down to size and work up a good sweat in the process. Jeffrey was gorgeous, and when he began to fuck me, I discovered a happiness I'd never known. I begged him to move in, wanted him constantly, until he finally agreed. The yard went to hell after that. He took advantage of my generosity, but I didn't care because of that cock and mouth. I had to have him. Had to.

"And then came the squabbles, small at first, but gradually taking on a life of their own. He created issues between us, none of which I saw as relevant, and became hostile toward the life I gave him, finding fault at every turn. We entered a war of sorts, fucking our way through a minefield we ourselves had planted."

He stopped and I felt the shudder. He was crying again. I pulled him around to face me and took him into my arms. Sniffling, he finished the story. "I knew he wasn't faithful. I told myself that so long as he kept me satisfied, I could live with it, but in the end, I couldn't and we again had terrible fights. That's when he left me. The last time he fucked me, he already had his bags packed. I didn't know it at the time; I discovered it afterward. It was the ultimate humiliation."

He pulled a wrist up between us and said, "I didn't do it right. Up, not across, someone told me, later on."

I took his hand between mine and felt him at last begin to settle. When he looked into my eyes, I kissed him, gently lingering. I felt a stir that was, for once, not my cock.

"What's your name?" he asked.

"Doug Reynolds."

"Doug. I like that. Such a hard, masculine sound to it. I'm Leland Cady."

"I know." I ran a hand through his hair. "I've seen all your films."

"Ah, yes, my films." He pulled back, and it felt like someone else had gotten into bed with us. "That's another life now, so remote. Everything stopped with Jeffrey. I was rather foolish."

"We all are sometimes."

He laughed. "Dear boy, thank you, but I doubt your foolishness could ever measure up to mine."

"Well, maybe not."

"Tell me about yourself, Doug. Do you fuck your other customers?"

"It's not the same," I said.

"Of course not, but tell me anyway."

We spent the rest of the afternoon together, eventually migrating out to the pool. I told him about servicing his neighbors. He pressed for details. It seemed to energize him as well as reassure him that he hadn't acted all that foolishly.

"Why don't you go for a swim?" he suggested. "You've kept the pool so clean, and nobody's using it."

"Come in with me."

"I can't swim," he said. "Let me sit and watch. I'll enjoy it far more."

We remained naked and, as I slid into the water, he settled back in a chair, where he seemed almost content. I, in turn, made a show for him, loving every minute. Everything I did was meant to please him, and so I moved through the water with all the grace I could muster, conscious of him watching my ass as it broke the surface, my cock when I floated on my back. Paddling gently with my left hand, I stroked myself with my right. I looked over to see Leland smiling, lost in a world I think he feared he'd never regain.

I soon gave up the pool job and moved in with him, learning what it was like to live for one man. I became Leland's lover, friend, and live-in fan. He became my everything.

For a long while, I was content, probably because we never

really looked up from what we were doing. We passed days naked and fucking to near oblivion. It amazed me how much he needed, almost as if he wasn't alive without a cock inside him. We went from fucking to making love and back again, wonderful wild escapades that took us into the garden or out beside the pool, then quiet sensual interludes in bed. He told me over and over how much he loved me, and I heard myself say much the same in return, gradually opening to him, letting him touch the soft center. I'd never experienced anything so all encompassing, and I ached for his presence, his wonderfully passive power.

We enjoyed four glorious months before our first scene.

I thought I knew him, but found, on that fateful day, that I'd been harboring an illusion. Leland had never professed to be anything but what he was: an actor. I was the one who read things into him, who decided his need for me and his declarations of love were genuine. How naive.

In the mornings, I always awakened to find him curled against me, snoring lightly. Hair tousled, first blond bristle at his chin, he would raise in me an incredible need, and I'd fuck him awake. He would always play to it, allowing me the illusion of sleep, even as his cock erupted. Now, for the first time, I was alone in bed. My initial thought was of some game, him hiding in the hall, wanting to be chased. I rolled out of bed fully erect and went to find him.

Annoyed when I discovered he wasn't in the house, I barged out onto the patio and saw him among the fruit trees with a beautiful dark-haired young man I knew to be the gardener. Jeffrey's replacement, I thought, feeling a twinge, because I considered that role mine.

I didn't hesitate in my nakedness, even though they were dressed, probably because Leland had on the same white shirt and slacks he'd worn that first day with me. I tried not to read anything into it as I approached. My cock, however, grew heavier with each step, engorged with anger as well as blood.

"Doug, this is Troy," Leland sang as I drew near. "He's doing wonders with the trees, don't you think?"

I didn't answer. I stepped behind Leland, slid my arms around him, and shoved my prick between his legs. "Troy, this is Doug, who you've undoubtedly seen around the pool."

I was grinding against Leland's ass while looking past him at the intruder who couldn't have been more than twenty and who wore nothing but a pair of ragged khaki cutoffs and scuffed brown boots.

"Where are your manners, Doug?" Leland cooed, clearly enjoying the attentions of not one but two young men. As he spoke, he drew his legs together and began to squeeze, and I realized then he'd be perfectly happy bringing me off while engaged in the idlest chat. My cockhead was visible to Troy, who was unable to keep his eyes off it, stumbling with his words and failing to answer Leland's questions about the trees.

"Come inside," I said into Leland's ear.

"And miss this gorgeous morning?" he replied. "No, let's stay out here and watch Troy tame mother nature."

I pulled back and spun him around. "What's going on?" I demanded.

He gave me a puzzled look, smiling indulgently as he might to a wayward child, and said, "Troy is trimming the trees and I am supervising. I would think that obvious."

"If you don't come into the house, I'm going to fuck you right here."

"You wouldn't!"

I wanted to slap him, to wrestle him to the ground and shove my dick so far up him he'd choke, but held back because I saw it was what he wanted, that he was purposely creating a scene.

"I would," I said, and though I meant it and had every intention of following through, I saw the mood had shifted, the balance of power now his. I was left with nothing but choice: play a part or allow the understudy my role.

"No!" Leland mocked, grinning at Troy. It was more dare than refusal, and I wondered, as I reached to unbutton his shirt, if he really thought me so dumb as to not see the manipulation. "Doug," he further protested, tone playful now. Troy stood transfixed, cock tenting his khakis.

I pulled away Leland's shirt, undid his pants, and let them drop. True to form, he wasn't aroused. He always needed to be brought along no matter how sexually charged, something I wrote off only partly to age. Control was a major factor, I was starting to see. He wanted to be done to, used, but he also wanted to get us onto his own personal stage.

When he was naked, he simply stood, and as much as I resented the choreographed mood, I still wanted him. Troy was biting his lip and the hand that had hung at his side now slid over to his crotch, where it began to prod. "Oh, Troy, dearest," Leland said. "Look at him, Doug, look at all that young promise. Why don't you get out of those things, Troy, take a break? It's all right, you can do the trees later."

Troy looked to me, but Leland intervened. "Do as I say, Troy. You work for me, not Doug."

Troy turned, studying Leland as if he hadn't seen him until that moment, gaze descending until settled on the limp cock. "Why don't you make it hard?" Leland suggested, and Troy drew a long, very audible breath, then stripped. "Oh dear," Leland exclaimed, drawing a hand to his mouth. "Look at him, Doug, look at that gorgeous prick, and so hard. Like a tree branch, isn't it? Our little gardener sporting a limb. Come here, dear boy. Come suck my cock."

I knew then what Leland had in mind, and I hated him for it. He smiled as Troy dropped to his knees, scooped the soft dick into his mouth, and began a spirited suck. The boy worked his own cock as he fed, and Leland looked over at me with such smugness, such triumph, that I wanted to flee or, no, wanted to pull the boy off and send him packing, then pummel Leland about the yard and fuck him until he couldn't breathe, until every drop of blood in his veins was down inside his cock and his heart ran dry and stopped. I thought of all this, but remained still, looking from Troy's bobbing head down to his frantic jerking, then up to Leland's grin.

That was something else I was learning, how Leland doled himself out, how he needed desperately to be taken, but gave so little in return. He was allowing the boy to get him hard, but offering not a twitch, not a hint of thrust, his cock like some Popsicle treat for the youngster.

"Fuck him," Leland said to me in a voice so calm, so sure, that I wouldn't have believed a blow job was in process had I not been witness. "While he's doing me," Leland added. "Go on. I'm sure you'll find a condom in his pocket."

I don't know if Troy heard any of this. He was slurping with such enthusiasm that I doubt he knew or cared what was taking place around him, and then, all at once, he was spraying jizz. Pumping in a frenzy, he kept on after he'd spent and soon was hard again. For a second, I envied him.

The condom was there, and I suited up, then Leland gently pulled Troy off him. "Over here, sweetie," he said, and guided Troy to a mat beside the pool. Troy, hand still on his prong, followed obediently and allowed Leland to position him on all fours. Leland then sank to his knees, thrust his now stiff dick back into Troy's mouth, looked at me, and nodded.

I hesitated, confusion washing over me. The ass was pink and ripe, balls tight in their sack, lightly fuzzed. I'd never refused such an offering, but now actually considered it, wanting Leland instead, Leland who I loved, Leland who had become my everything. I looked at him and found him watching me. "Do it," he commanded, and when I still hesitated, he added, "for me."

I shook my head no; he nodded yes. And we spent a few seconds in an awful mime before I lost patience and shoved my cock into Troy's ass. He flinched as I dug my fingers into his hips to keep him anchored, then began to plow him with all I had. I heard him gasp, and he dropped Leland's cock for a second, issued a squeal, then quieted and let Leland guide the dick back into his mouth.

The rise I felt didn't belong to me; it was Leland's, and he acknowledged it with outstretched arms, as if playing to an audience he no longer had, basking in thunderous applause. Trapped in the scene, I went wild and began to thrust so hard into Troy that he nearly lost his balance. When a climax beckoned, Leland knew it. "Come for me, Doug," he coached. "Come for Troy. Get up inside him and let go the way you do in me."

"Shit," I growled as it began. Ass, thighs, balls, cock, everything drawing up then firing, the pulse so intense I cried out with each spurt, not caring who in the hell I was fucking. It was so good, so goddamned good, and afterward, as I gasped for breath, I had to wonder if the fact that Leland had orchestrated it made a difference. I'd never done him this good. All the times I'd fucked him, pumping that incredible ass, I'd never had it like this. And I saw that he knew it. He grinned at me, pulled out of Troy's mouth, took his cock in hand, and began to come, shooting over Troy's shoulder onto his back. Leland never made a sound as he unloaded, he just kept looking at me, as if we were sharing the act, as if Troy hadn't been between us.

Troy collapsed on the mat and rolled onto his side while I discarded the condom and waited. Leland got to his feet, ignoring

Troy now. "Let's go inside," he said, reaching down to fondle my prick. I was stunned by his assumption and choked back an onslaught of words. I wanted to tell him he couldn't do this, that he was killing something inside me, something just born that hadn't had enough time to breathe, but instead I pushed him away.

"You're not taking this seriously, are you?" he said, as if love were some kind of aberration. I realized then how he'd ruined me, how he'd gotten into places previously off limits and was tramping about for his own amusement, feeding the actor's insatiable ego and turning me back into the hustler I'd once been.

"Actually, I take it very seriously," I said, and I left him there and went inside to pack.

DUE DILIGENCE

Rhidian Brenig Jones

I liked to fuck older men. Not the real crumblies—liver spots and prostate problems didn't do it for me—but guys in their forties, now that was a different ball game. My ex, Derry, reckoned I had a father complex, but what did he know? A ten-week course from some online college and he was a shrink? To be clear, I didn't have anything against the Daddy/son thing—short of scat and kids, whatever floats your boat, I say.

Take Peter, my forty-five-year-old. A nice enough guy—pitiful acorn cock, but we can't all be hung—who liked to splash his hand in the arc of my piss. Not a problem unless I'd hit rush hour and my bladder had expanded to the size of a beach ball by the time he was (slowly) unbuttoning my shirt. He asked once if I'd pee up his ass, but although his face fell, he didn't pursue it when I pointed out this would only flood the condom.

Then there was Stuart. He edged close to weird and even closer to fifty. He'd moan a certain name against my neck, over and over, in time with my thrusts. Turned out that *Matthew* had been his brother. Guy had broken his neck taking an ill-advised dive into three feet of water off a rock in Cornwall.

Gerard. Martin. Poor John, a ferocious bottom whose shaved skull and cropped beard gave the impression that his face had been put on upside down.

All of them with needs, all desperate to indulge their little kinks. And, of course, all desperate to pay me.

My fellow post-grads might have opted to juggle minimum-wage McJobs and crushing hours in the lab in an attempt to peel a few quid off their debt mountains, but I intended to complete my doctorate *in the black*. Fuck my way to solvency.

So why older men? It wasn't that I couldn't get it up for Generation Z—god knows, energy and a twenty-minute refractory period have their place—but vigor isn't everything. Maturity was the real turn-on for me. Still is. The strength, the confidence, the assured self-possession of a silverback in the fullness of his power. Heavily built, maybe a little healthy fat overlying solid muscle. As my Welsh aunties used to cackle, bookending me on the sofa as we watched the rugby, *a nice bit of* gafael *to get your hands on*.

When I'd first ventured into the world of negotiable affections, I'd fucked indiscriminately, building my business by taking on anyone who could afford me, but a mounting bank balance had allowed me to cull the herd, and I'd reduced my clients to a carefully considered three.

Dayal was a cardiothoracic surgeon at the university hospital, a tall Sikh with aquamarine eyes and a cut-glass accent whose ex-wife had produced two sets of twins in four years and yet was still sleeping with him out of guilt; I reckoned I'd be giving the gal a rest. Then there was Patrick, who owned a wholesale food business as well as a couple of fine-dining restaurants, which translated to fifty quid for three slivers of rare-breed pork and a heritage carrot on a plate the size of a cartwheel—not that I ever had to pay, mind you. Last but not least, my favorite. Elliott was a senior banker in the City, a big man in more ways than one. I wasn't entirely sure what mergers and acquisitions actually involved, but he was doing bloody well on it if a Docklands penthouse and a vintage DB6 were anything to go by. Elliott wasn't as handsome as Dayal, or as lighthearted as Patrick, but he was sophisticated, seriously smart, and I found his rugged masculinity insanely attractive. He was demanding in bed, but a generous fuck nevertheless, although it could have been that he intensified his own orgasms by holding back to watch my ring constrict his cock as I came.

I'd been falling for Elliott for some time. Falling heavily. I wasn't sure what I felt for him, but if it wasn't love, it was its first cousin.

That particular night, he'd hooked a leg over my thigh. Sleepy in the languorous aftermath of a marathon session, I'd stroked silkily down, roughly up against the grain of hair as he stirred lazy fingers in my bush. As always, I'd yearned to feel his arms around me, holding me against the warm expanse of his chest, but he never wanted to cuddle, and I knew better than to ask.

He ran a finger along my exhausted prick and I murmured regretfully, "I don't think I could. Not yet."

"Not that. I want to ask you something."

"Mmm?"

His finger stilled and then resumed its movement. "How many men do you fuck?"

I'd stiffened, and not in a good way. "Why do you ask?"

"I'm curious."

"Obviously, but why?"

"Just answer me."

I'd discounted Christopher because I did him pro bono. The poor sod was losing his sight to some early-onset degenerative condition, and most of the time he simply wanted to peer at my erection, his head tilted like a bird's as he struggled to fix the picture, a memory to draw on for when his world became dark. "Three."

"Two too many."

Frowning, I'd flattened the pillow under my cheek so that I could see his face. "What d'you mean?"

He'd moved his hand to the undercurve of my ass. "I understand why you do what you do. Makes a kind of sense. But from now on, I want this kept only for me. Exclusive use."

My heart had soared with jubilation. *Oh, Christ, was he saying* . . . ?

"I know you need the money. I'm assuming your other clients pay what I do? How would it be if I covered the loss?"

"I don't understand."

"I don't let anyone else drive my car, so why would I want anyone else fucking my whore?"

Whore. The word stabbed in my guts, but that's what I was. Ludicrous to imagine he'd meant what I wanted him to mean. I'd swallowed the resentment I'd felt, and said, "You'd pay what I would have had from them? Is that what you're saying?"

"Isn't that what all the *grandes horizontales* wanted, to be kept by one man?"

"Wrong gender."

"Don't nitpick." He'd stroked my ass. "This. Your mouth, your cock. All for me."

"Can I ask *you* something?"

He'd seemed surprised that I hadn't instantly bitten his hand off. "If you want. Don't promise to answer, though."

"It's just . . . why d'you pay for sex? There must be a million men out there who'd give their left bollock to be . . . to have . . ."

"A relationship with me?"

"Well, yes."

His expression had hardened. "A relationship with my money, more like."

"Oh, come on."

He'd chewed at the corner of his lip. "Let's just say, I've seen too many pound signs *ker-ching* in too many eyes. I need sex, need to fuck, but on my terms. I don't need emotional baggage, don't need so-called romance, and I *really* don't need to be wondering whether it's me or the thought of my wallet that's getting a guy off. I want a straightforward business transaction, so everyone knows where they stand."

No warmth, no affection. A cold detachment instead of the passionate connectedness that can transform a physical act into something transcendent, so much more than the simple purging of semen. He'd been hurt; I would have cherished him. The sad bubble of hope that had remained to me had finally broken with a forlorn little pop. "Absolutely. I see that."

He'd given my hip a teasing pinch. "Well, you would. Eye on the main chance. Another thing. There might be times when I'd want you with me at social events, dinners, things like that. A pretty boy on my arm to keep the vultures off. Your usual fee. Well? What d'you say?"

I'd forced a brilliant smile and folded his fingers around my cock. "All yours."

Not that I'd meant it: no way I'd slaughter two out of three cash cows. Elliott had made his position clear. I was no more than a commodity to be traded like coffee or copper or fucking soybeans. There was no guarantee that the thing with him would go the distance; it was a buyer's market and a new, improved version of The Great British Whore could emerge at any time. I'd felt vaguely uncomfortable at the thought of cheating him, but it would have been crazy to put all my eggs in one basket. There was a tiny risk that he'd discover my double-dealing, but the odds were well in my favor. The three of them worked in different sectors, lived in different parts of London, moved in different spheres. Their paths were unlikely to cross. There was no reason they'd ever come within a mile of one another.

A few weeks into our little arrangement, I'd worked until well after midnight and only returned home when the numbers began to blur. So I was semi-comatose when I fumbled for my phone at seven in the morning.

"Yeah."

"Did I wake you?"

Shit! I shot upright and cleared my dry throat. "Pity you weren't here to do it."

He gave the throaty grunt of laughter that always went straight to my balls. "Late night?"

"In the lab."

"Ah. Look, I won't keep you. Thing is, I'm having people over for drinks on Friday evening. I know it's short notice, but I was wondering if you'd be free."

I smiled, thrilled at the thought. "Should be fine."

"Good. About half past eight. See you then."

"Elliott, just a sec. Who am I? Who should I be?"

"Oh yes, of course. Sorry. Uh . . . business associate."

Business associate? Childishly disappointed, I pulled a sulky face at the phone. "See you then."

He lived in a duplex penthouse in St. Katherine's Dock, although, in a rare confiding moment, he'd let slip that he planned to move out to the Green Belt at some point. The commute would be hell, but more than offset by a couple of leafy acres in Bucks or Berks. I'm a city boy, and rustic has never appealed, but I'd have been happy with a basement in Clacton if he was in it. The lift pinged and I took a last look at myself, smoothing my hair and baring my teeth at the mirror. I didn't think we'd end up fucking, but I'd prepared as meticulously as always, just in case. Squeaky clean inside and out, a misting of Dior Homme at the base of my spine, but no deodorant because he liked to suck my pits. I was wearing clinging, icing-sugar white trunks, fresh out of the box, under navy Paul Smith and an Armani cashmere crew neck.

"Wow." Hanging on to the door to his apartment, he swept his gaze over me and gave a whistle of appreciation. His gaze dropped to my mouth and, for a startled second, I thought he'd welcome me with a kiss instead of a white envelope stuffed with twenties, but he merely tilted his head and waved me ahead of him.

Surprised, I looked around the empty room and asked, "Am I early?"

"They're nosing about upstairs." He walked to the foot of the staircase. "*Guys!*"

Two sets of feet appeared, descending the spiral. Trouser legs, jacket hems . . . they reached the bottom and I felt the blood leave my head.

Behind me, Elliott massaged my shoulders, fingers digging painfully above my collarbones. "I've been having you watched. Did you really think I wouldn't check? Due diligence, Jesse. One of the keys to business success," he whispered over the curve of my ear. "We had a very interesting conversation about you over crab with white truffle, so I don't think introductions are necessary."

Patrick simply stared, but Dayal put his wineglass down and smiled, his eyes glacial. I twisted out of Elliott's grip, but when I made to move past him, he sidestepped and blocked my way. When I saw the expression on his face, I felt a spurt of real fear.

I held up my hands. "Okay, you've got me. Nice one. So, if—"

Elliott said, "No need to rush off. Dayal, a drink for our friend."

"No, look, I don't—"

"Of course you do." He extended an arm. "Please."

My heart hammering, I crossed the floor and sat stiffly on one of the Mies van der Rohe chairs. The cream one. I'd Googled it once; the thing had cost more than my car. Patrick pushed a glass into my hand and, after a moment, I took a gulp. The velvety Bordeaux slipped down like battery acid.

"Now then," Elliott said, leaning an elbow on the mantel, "it seems that our agreement must have slipped your mind. You do remember it, don't you? You know, when I offered to cover your losses if you'd reserve yourself for me? A bit of a facer for Patrick and Dayal, losing your services and all that, but they're big boys, and sluts like you are two a penny. Well, not quite two a penny, but you know what I mean. Remind me how many times he's fleeced me, guys?"

"Once," Dayal murmured.

"Three," Patrick offered, raising his eyebrows at Dayal's look of surprise. "Hey, he's bloody good. Hole like a pressure bandage."

"Hardly the simile I'd have chosen, but each to his own. So, four times at seven-fifty a throw. Not a staggering amount, but I don't appreciate being scammed out of a penny."

I gave him a sick smile. "Elliott, I'll pay you back. All of it."

"And how do you propose to do that?"

"Not straightaway, but once I qualify. There's a research post coming up at UCL, and I'm in with a good chance of getting it."

"Not anymore you're not. I had a word with your head of department this morning."

I went cold. *Oh, Jesus fuck . . .*

"Professor de Stefano. Nice guy, isn't he? We discussed your little sideline. I felt I had to warn him. Warn him, you know, about the risk of letting something like you loose among his students. Vulnerable, impressionable kids, some of them not even eighteen. Imagine the effect on the university's reputation once that got out. Doesn't bear thinking about. So, I reckon you can kiss UCL goodbye. You'll be lucky to get a job sweeping floors in Home Bargains with the reference de Stefano'll give you now. He'll be emailing you. He wants to see you, first thing tomorrow morning."

They say you see your whole life flash before your eyes, but it wasn't my past I saw. All I saw was the smoking wreck of my future. I held my head in my hands as panic threatened to overwhelm me.

Dayal's voice broke through the roaring in my ears. "You reap what you sow, Jesse, you reap what you sow."

My lips were numb. "He didn't have to do that. There was no need for that."

"Think yourself lucky we didn't call the police."

I shook my head and swiped at my cheeks with the heels of my hands. They came away wet. I was still staring at them in confusion when a sound brought my head up.

Patrick was biting his knuckles to stifle his laughter. Dayal's mouth was quirked in amusement. Elliott was unreadable.

It took slow seconds for understanding to dawn, for me to realize how completely I'd been had.

Elliott jerked his chin. "Joke's over. Get up."

The surge of relief was so intense it made my head swim. Patrick and Dayal strolled to the door and, after a few muttered words, Elliott closed it behind them.

"You bastard. I didn't deserve that. Whatever you think, I didn't deserve that."

"You reckon? You should be bloody grateful I didn't carry it through. Tell me," he said, picking up his glass, "just before you fuck off, in what way was my offer not good enough?"

My legs were still too shaky to support me, so I stayed where
I was.

"Well?"

It wasn't as if telling the truth would make things any worse.
"It wasn't what I wanted, so I took what I could get."

He glared, dark eyes wide and hateful. "So, what the fuck *did*
you want?"

The pool of humiliation that had been simmering in my gut
erupted in a boiling geyser of rage. "You! Not your money! You!
But you couldn't see it, could you, because a whore doesn't have
feelings—"

"Feelings? Jesus, that's a good one! What feelings? Greed?
Deceit? Betrayal? All the—"

"*I love you, you stupid prick!*"

Speechless in the strangling silence, we stared at each other
until I dropped my eyes. The curl of his lip told me what I needed
to know, and all I wanted then was to crawl back under my rock
without getting any more salt poured on me. I started to move
toward the door.

"Jesse, wait."

"If it's about the money, I told you, I'll pay you back."

"It's not about the money."

"Then there's nothing more to be said."

"I think there is. Couldn't you trust me to keep my side of the
bargain?"

I rubbed fingers and thumb together in a *money-money* gesture.
"I'm a whore. The only thing I trust is my bank balance."

"Crap. There's got to be more to you than that, surely to
Christ."

Anger drained out of me, leaving me simply tired. "Oh, there's
more. Thing is, you can't see it."

He considered me. "You said once that I could have anyone

I wanted. Maybe I could. So why you, Jesse? Haven't you ever wondered why I chose you?"

I found it difficult to speak over the tightness in my throat. Hope was the killer and I *would not* let him hurt me again. I shrugged. "Because I make you come like a grenade's going off in your balls."

For the first time that evening he gave an unguarded smile. "True." He walked up to me, coming so close that I smelled the wine on his breath. "But I can do that for myself. An hour with a fleshlight and a string of beads . . ."

Hope was the terrible ache in my chest. Hope was the rocketing of my pulse. Hope was the killer. "Don't, Elliott."

Huskily, he whispered, "Don't what, baby?"

Endearment was the killer.

"Didn't you ever think I might have feelings, too, you avaricious, mercenary, lying little shit?"

"Why would I? You said you weren't looking for—"

"I know what I said. Forget what I said." He ran a finger slowly over my bottom lip. "There're things we're going to have to talk about, but I think there's been enough talking for now, don't you?"

I touched as I had always wanted to, not to arouse him, but to please myself. I knew his cock—it was almost as familiar to me as my own. The broad head, pale mauve, distended with blood; the generous folds of foreskin; the straight, smooth shaft. I knew the heft of his balls. I knew the clean musk of his perineum and the texture of his pubic hair. But there were other places, other parts of his body. I kissed the tenderness of his eyelids, and licked at the fan of creases at the junction of torso and arm. My forefinger felt sharp edges of teeth and the little palatal ridges behind. Supine, eyes half-closed, he let me explore.

Elliott's chest was such a turn-on that the sexual tension in my cock threatened to split it open. The dark pelt, the hard planes of muscle, *the flatness* made me shudder with desire. He held my head as I suckled, pressing me close. I imagined those stiff little nipples spurting semen onto my tongue.

He shifted and eased my face up. I propped myself on one elbow and kissed his fingers as he gently palmed my chin free of saliva. Cupping my jaw, very quietly, very solemnly, he asked, "Will you fuck me, Jesse?"

The first time I'd sucked him, I'd slid my hand from his balls to the cleft of his ass, but he'd jackknifed away with a curt "Not there!" and the area had been forbidden territory ever since. When I could control my voice, I said, "You've never wanted that before."

"Things are different now. I want you in me, fucking the spunk out of me." I squeezed the frenum of my cock, hard, and frantically multiplied prime numbers in my head. "But go easy; it's been ages."

I kissed him, hard and deep and slow, giving his nose a reassuring bump with mine as I drew away. "Lift your legs."

He raised them, gripping his shins, and I knelt between his thighs. I'd never seen his hole, and even with his legs spread in a wide V, there was still hair to contend with. I brushed, stroking until I exposed the opening. It pulled inward, clenching reflexively as I caressed, velvety soft, a little sticky with sweat, redolent of the divine scent of male ass. I licked from coccyx to perineum, and pressed my fingertips against his rim to open him. Shell-pink flesh, soft and glistening, engulfed my tongue in salty-sourness, as his cock jumped and quivered on his belly.

He wasn't as tight as I thought he'd be. Once I'd lubed him, my fingers slid easily, and I could tell from his groans that the gentle stretching gave him only pleasure, no pain. Nevertheless, I murmured, "You like this? The way I'm doing it?"

"Deeper in."

I was careful to avoid stimulating his prostate. His cock was leaking heavily, and the sight of my fingers in his ass had brought mine to hair-trigger sensitivity. I didn't want either of us to come when I was outside his body. I slithered out and then fitted the condom.

"Ready, handsome?"

"Yes."

I entered him in one slow, slick glide, easing into the depths of him, something I'd done countless times, but always to others and never like this. Never with ardor, never with love. We kissed, my tongue delving as deeply into his mouth as my cock strained into his ass. He locked his ankles at the base of my spine and I began a slow rocking, more a tensing of my groin than thrusting. I wanted him to feel the intense pressure, and the stretch, the exquisite pleasure of being penetrated that he'd denied himself for so long. But he tightened his asshole, grabbing my cock like a fist, and I drove in, in and out, overwhelmed by the primal need to *fuck*. I withdrew, almost entirely out, held there, held there, still in control. Until he whispered, "Jesse . . ." Until he jerked his pelvis and bit my neck, and I was gone.

I heard his cry and felt the slippery flood of his semen on my belly. Blind, lost, I surrendered to the rapture of climax, and came and came.

"When's your oral, for the PhD?"

I'd forgotten about the bloody exam. I blew out an apprehensive breath. "A fortnight Tuesday."

"How does it work? Do they tell you there and then?"

"They send you out of the room while they confer, then call you back in. It's usually fine, pending corrections. There are always corrections, major or minor. A nice way is to be called back in and have the external examiner shake your hand and say, "Congratulations, Dr. Whatever."

He slid his arm around my waist and pulled me to cuddle against him. I could hear the beat of his heart, the steady thump under my cheek. I could smell the semen I hadn't let him clean away.

"Think you'll be okay?"

"Yeah, should be."

"Dr. Nicholl. Sounds good. It has a ring to it."

"I've been practicing writing it."

"Have you?"

"No."

He laughed and I felt a sinking sense of loss. Loss and regret for the pain we'd caused each other. He'd frightened me witless, but I'd been no better than the grasping sods who'd bent this gorgeous man out of shape. "Elliott, I'm sorry. For what I did. I'm really sorry."

"Forget it."

I looked up at him. "Did you really think about telling the prof?"

"Don't be absurd. We were pissed off and we wanted to teach you a lesson, that's all. Seems to have had an effect." He stroked my back. "So, will the newly qualified Dr. Nicholl be carrying on with his ancillary job?"

"Christ, no."

"I might have some work for you, if you're interested."

"I'm going to be focusing on my academic career from now on. I want to pay you back with honest money."

"I don't need you to pay me back, and anyway, it's not paid work."

I rested my hand on his chest, watching its slow rise and fall. "Oh?"

"I'm still looking for a guy to deter the vultures."

The burst of warmth blooming inside me made me grin like an idiot. "You mean you won't be telling me to bugger off?"

"It'll be a boost to my ego to have a research scientist as my 'plus one.' Impress the intellectual snobs. Mr. Challoner and his partner, Dr. Nicholl. What d'you think?"

"Elliott, you don't need any boosts to your ego, but . . ." I hovered, making him wait for the kiss. "I think it's got a *fine* ring to it."

RENAISSANCE MIRACLES

Michael Ampersant

Luigi took me aside this morning and said that, however much he enjoys our *leetle* get-togethers, he can no longer—despite his best efforts and my best efforts—hide the absence of any payments toward Room 312 from the all-knowing reservation system of the Savoy Palace Hotel. He fussed with a drawer and held up his credit card. "*Here*," he said, under his breath, "go to the Via de' Tornabuoni, buy yourself a new outfit, and take up position on the steps of the Loggia della Signoria. That should solve your *leetle* problems, pretty boy that you are. But don't forget to return the credit card first."

He then looked left and right, the way Italian hotel managers look left and right before getting a blow job, waved me to his side of the reception counter, and there we went again: me squatting in the hollow space under the desk accommodating his Italian dick, and him accommodating a new guest, a *contessa,* apparently.

I'm a slut. Meaning, fortunately, I can handle this.

And that's why I'm here on the steps of the Loggia sitting next to the marble statue of Cellini's Perseus, me a wannabe hustler with a boyfriend who, suddenly, last month, discovered his passion for the Tuscan Renaissance and begged me to take him to Florence, where he would study with a certain Professore Pellegrino, a mysterious art historian—whom I still haven't met.

So I took Jamie to Florence in the hope that our challenged, floundering relationship would see its own Renaissance amidst the marble willies on the statues there, but—I don't know what it is, perhaps the marble willies are too small—the fact is, we haven't had sex since our arrival, and now we've also run out of money. And yet—despite the slut that I am—I'm still hopelessly in love with him. He's so beautiful, downright angelic in fact.

And there we are, me sporting an A&F-branded T-shirt, Apennine leather shorts, and Buttero running shoes. I shouldn't give the impression of a rent boy, obviously, so I'm absorbed by my iPhone and take pictures of a crazed woman dressed up like Mae West walking four dogs amidst the three hundred people that populate the Piazza della Signoria this spring morning—half of them tourists in sneakers, one quarter Italian (heels, patent leather shoes), and the rest undefined. Undefined is what I need, of course, as I've discovered a weakness for budding billionaires with a sense of humor and time on their hands. None of them is in evidence, regrettably, so I take more pictures. I snap the idle horse cabs waiting for tourists, and the patina-infested Poseidon, which is the main statue of the fountain on the corner of the Palazzo Vecchio.

A black guy has materialized next to the fountain and is taking pictures of the Loggia. Meaning, he's taking pictures of me taking pictures of him taking pictures of me, and so on. There's a funny trade-off in this *if* it's a come-on—but who's coming on to whom? Whether the guy is actually aware of my existence remains to be seen—the Loggia, after all, accommodates a dozen statues and three dozen sightseers—but I'm feeling increasingly aware of him, especially down under in my Apennine leather shorts.

He's the Kenyan type, long and stalky, ebony-black, clad in a half-open Hawaii shirt that leaves nothing to the imagination, wide strong shoulders, shiny tapered pecs, the torso funneling down to the small of his back along effortless abs. Obama-man has a beautiful, oval face, infinite lips, flaring nostrils, and wears stylish gray flannel pants, widely cut, much wider than would be the fashion on the Via de' Tornabuoni.

I know about these pants; guys wear them to hide their third leg.

I've stopped snapping; he's stopped snapping. If I get up now, he'll become aware of my Apennine leather bulge, and the result could go either way. I mean, with black folks you never know, especially with rich kids from Africa, in that they're all queer or none of them is, and they're either unfamiliar with the code of gay cruising or loath to use it.

In any case, before I can do anything, a thirtysomething man enters my field of vision, walks across the piazza, casts three glances in my direction, and acts as if he's interrupted by his cell phone.

Now then, there are two types of billionaires—according to literary fiction, going back to Tolstoy: unhappy billionaires, who are each unhappy in their own way, and happy billionaires with distinctive Roman noses, who answer "whatever" when their valet enquires as to today's attire, and are then fitted with a Bond Street summer costume in understated blue. Our man belongs to the second category.

I don't always get it right, but this time I do. Mr. Bond-Street has finished his phone conversation, makes a beeline for yours truly, and introduces himself as Giovanni. He speaks some English. He asks whether I like art.

"Real art. Botticelli. Da Vinci." He chuckles.

"Of course I like art."

"There's this museum around the corner, the Uffizi," he says. "Would you like to join me there?"

"No prob," I answer, and straighten my A&F-branded T-shirt and my dick. The Uffizi, after all, is the most important museum in the world (according to the local tourist guide, that is).

The museum's entrance is forty yards on the left side of the arcades, down to the Arno. In the summer, Giovanni tells me, lines extend kilometers in all directions. This is early season and the line is merely fifty yards long, but it doesn't matter. He walks us up to the entrance, and then—as if any proof is needed that he's the real thing, with three gym trainers on retainer—he rolls his shoulders and scoops me up with both arms as if I were a sick child. He asks the nearest tourist to lower the stanchion belt at the head of the queue. "*Pronto, emergencia!*" he says. "We have lives to save here!"

The entrance doors slide open. Inside, he sets me back on my feet, then fumbles in a pocket and issues an ID-badge. "*Pronto,*" he repeats, holding the badge up to the face of the first available museum guard. The guard grabs the ID and holds it to a ticketing machine. Like in airports, it's electronic, with a turnstile and a bar code reader. The badge is offered to the laser and we're in!

Hold on. There's an old-fashioned cloakroom, where tourists are supposed to leave their knapsacks. "This is what separates the *uomini* from the *ragazzi*," he explains. "We will become a piece of art, Emilio. Strip."

I look at him. I'm more boy than man, to translate, and my name isn't Emilio, but I nod just the same.

"*Sarebbe più facile se la gente lo registrasse,*" he addresses the crowd around us. "Folks, listen to me. We are contemporary art in the making. Activate your iPhones. Let's make history, *pronto.*"

Anglo-Saxons are seemingly delayed by suddenly hearing their own language thrown at them, and other tourist nations dither, but Giovanni has already chucked his Bond-Street bottoms. He's turned his hirsute butt to the audience and folds his lower garments ceremoniously. He hands the stack to the cloak woman. She hands him a numbered badge in return. He's facing me. "*Arte*, Emilio," he says. "*Belissimo*."

I follow his example. "*Ahh*," the crowd goes, mainly because I'm quite pretty, plus, when you're barely legal age and drop your pants, people pay attention.

Giovanni hands my Apennine shorts to the cloak woman and takes my hand. "Let's make history," he reaffirms. "*Correre!* Run!"

"Emilio?" I throw at him while we're flying down the corridors past all the marble statues with their tiny willies—and Roman noses.

"Emilio!" he answers. "That's your name, *non è vero?*"

"Yes," I say. FYI, my name is Dex.

"*The Annunciation*," he says, "*d'accordo?* Under *The Annunciation?*"

The Annunciation, I'm thinking. There are hundreds of them in Florence, according to the tourist guide—paintings of archangel Gabriel announcing to Mary that she would conceive and give birth to a son, Jesus. Five of them are in the Uffizi, and we are heading for the major one on the second floor, a work by Leonardo da Vinci.

Sinistra, Giovanni says, *here*. There's a throng of people bulging in front of a side entrance. The commotion has followed us down the corridors, and there are shrieks, with more people raising their iThings. We turn left and find ourselves in a smallish room with five pictures, two of which I remember.

Yes, there it hangs, a perfect double square of a canvas with an angelic Gabriel looking much like Jamie, and Maria behind an otherworldly work unit, half crystal ball, half laptop, taking notes. Well, at least that's what it looks like to me.

Giovanni hands his jacket to the guard.

"The painting is shielded by the panel," he says, "but let's not quibble. We owe this to history!" He points at the picture. "Never been done before!"

The guard doesn't seem to grasp what's going on—which makes two of us. He's grabbed Giovanni's jacket, holding it up like a smelly rag while fumbling with his Nokia phone, calling for help, apparently. So Giovanni grabs a bottle of water from the hands of a passing tourist and smashes it against the red-framed emergency alarm on the wall. The *RING* is ear-blowing and immediate. Overhead lights dim, emergency lights come on. Da Vinci's painting, I wonder, what is it worth on the holy markets?

Giovanni has clutched me from behind and moves into position. *"Pronto?"* he asks. I nod. "Fuck," he yells, and there we go: him throwing his thrusts, plunging and pumping, people recording this for posterity, and me moaning for the general benefit of the audience. We are half-serious. It matters little that I don't feel anything.

"Let's keep this going," he hollers. *"Ti piace?"*

"Ti piace? I don't understand," I say.

"You like it?" he hollers. *"Ti piace?"*

"Si, si," people answer, still holding up their iThings. *"Prendi la figa."*

"I can go on forever, you know!" Giovanni yells.

"Show us," a lonely skeptic heckles, but everybody else is making history by recording it.

"Fuck, fuck, fuck," Giovanni goes, and I echo obligingly with, "Fuck, fuck, fuck." I still don't feel anything.

"Fuck, fuck, fuck," people go.

It would be a pity for Giovanni to come *in obscura* with half the world watching, and so he quits at the *momento suprèmo*, and grabs his dinger. The lonely skeptic laughs. Other people laugh. "What is it?" I ask myself, trying to get a better view of Giovanni's equipment. And now the penny drops: I didn't feel anything since there was nothing to feel with Giovanni's microscopic willie up my ass. Although, I have to hand it to him, he's saving the moment, come-wise, with abundant cream spouting from his undersized manhood, and now splashing against the bulletproof glass pane protecting da Vinci's priceless art. So much jizz from so little to show. It's a Renaissance miracle and deserves the applause from a transfixed audience.

Giovanni raises his right hand in an old-fashioned V-gesture. "Listen, folks," he cries. "Don't hesitate to mail your clips to the VOLPE ADULT CHANNEL. V*olpe-dot-com.*" Another *V*-gesture is offered. "*Molto Grazie.* Thank you. Good-bye."

Quickly, before we can be arrested, he's retrieved his jacket from the guard, who's still fumbling with his cell phone, and we've descended the stairs and collected our belongings. Minutes later, we're sitting down for a postcoital drink on the patio of the Gucci Café. Giovanni pulls out his checkbook, asks for my real name, and signs a money order to the value of a hundred thousand Euro. "Don't you worry," he says, "this is just one percent of what I'll be making on our *leetle* art as the owner of Volpe TV, which I bought just this morning."

And that, as they say, is that. Until it's not.

I hurry home—if you can call a hotel a home—eager to settle the Savoy Palace bill once and for all. Luigi, the reception manager, is still on duty. I hand him the check. He raises his brows. "*Giovanni di Cristallo,*" he reads. "A mineral water? Let's see for sure." His eyes travel to a small, yet loquacious toy robot that sits on the reception desk and doubles as digital reader for Savoy's all-knowing reservation system. Luigi presents the check to the reader.

"*Ah, ah, ah,*" the toy robot snickers. "*Ah, ah, ah. Giovanni di Cristallo.* Another mineral water."

"I knew it," Luigi exclaims, trying not to snicker himself.

"What is it," I ask. "Anything wrong with the check?"

"Cristallo . . . well, the name is new, at least," he answers, "but it gives him away. He used to call himself Fabia, or Grazia, or Sparea." He frowned my way. "He sports a distinctive Roman nose, *non è vero?*"

"Yes."

"Still quite young? Fuckable, if provisions are made for the nose? Dressed like a billionaire in Bond-Street fashion?"

"Yes."

"He is an impostor, a poseur. But he is more than this when he rises to the occasion; he becomes a true make-belief artist, comparable to someone in the tradition of Houdini, Ponzi, and Donaldo Trump." He nods. "Believe me."

"He makes his money as an impostor?"

"The old-fashioned way. He spent three months in our hotel not paying a cent—room and board and martinis and come and everything—well, you know how it is. I still remember his nose on my underbelly. I'm a bit ticklish. *Meravigliosa*. That was before we got the new reservation system."

"Well," I say, "he didn't make any money from me."

"What did he do, then?"

I tell him the Uffizi story.

"*Mmmh,*" he says, tapping his fingers on the reception counter. "A new beesiness model. Wouldn't have worked fifteen years ago, when people still frowned upon smuttiness and raunch. But these days? Grab them by the pussy. The *Volpe* network, you say? Never heard of it." He shakes his head in disbelief. "And right under *The Annunciation!* Artful intercourse is all the rage. A brilliant idea. A brilliant guy, I told you." He grips my arm and rolls his eyes the way Italian hotel managers roll their eyes. "If I were you, I would be careful, though. Giovanni has a dark side. You had a chance to observe his anatomical peculiarity during your leetle get-together under *The Annunciation*, yes?"

"You mean that nose of his?" I ask, disingenuously.

"You know what I mean," Luigi replies. "A problem not

uncommon in Florence. With all those Renaissance willies around us, many a young man develops a penis complex so profound that he becomes unable to unfold his *virilia* into distinctive proportions. You understand?"

"Yes. No."

"But Giovanni," Luigi continues, "has turned his complex into a twisted, nay perverted, advantage. He poses as a sexologist on the Internet, promising healing to youngsters with erotic and relational afflictions. If he finds a taker, he invites the lad to Florence and fills him up with talk as to how true satisfaction is best achieved with very smallish organs. *Capici?*"

"Yes," I sigh.

"And then he proceeds to therapeutic practice, with himself as the coach. He even makes them pay, his victims."

Luigi is interrupted by a tall, black figure that has materialized next to me and has handed him a photograph, the picture of an unmistakable bulge covered in Apennine leather. And, yes, it's the Kenyan guy from this morning. "Have you seen this gentleman?" Obama-man asks, not yet aware that I'm standing a foot away. Luigi casts an appreciative glance at the bulge in the photo and offers it to the reader-robot of his reservation system.

"*All-knowing,*" Luigi confides to the African in conspiratorial tones. "Our reservation *seestem. Artefeecial Intelligence.*"

"*Ah, ah, ah,*" the robot snickers. "*Ah, ah, ah.* It is Dex! A nonpaying guest of our profit-challenged establishment. He's standing next to you, sir, this Dex of yours."

Luigi lowers his eyebrows. All of us do.

"Jamie," I whisper sideways to him. "Where's Jamie?"

Luigi dithers, then whispers back, "He went out." He then straightens his shoulders. "Anything you need *upstairs?*" he asks. His eyes travel from me to the African and back again.

"No," I reply.

Obama-man and I proceed to the elevator. It's a slow, profit-challenged elevator, and when we arrive at the third floor, the bulge in my shorts has reached Apennine proportions. "What's your name?" I ask him.

"Uume Mkubwa," he says. "Means . . . you'll see what it means."

The DO NOT DISTURB sign dangles on the knob of Room 312. *Strange*, I think, though not thinking further, as I always find it difficult to think in a state of advanced arousal. I wave my key-card and open the door.

Uume is the first to enter the room; I follow. Jamie—sweet, clever, angelic, untouchable Jamie is *not* out. He sits on the bed in his Calvin Kleins, his eyes traveling from Uume to my record bulge and back. Jamie knows that I'm into black skin. What can I say? "This is Uume," I say.

Jamie bursts into tears. I burst into tears. The end is near.

"You are friends?" Uume asks. "Lovers?"

"We were," Jamie answers.

"What happened?" Uume asks.

"Don't you see?" I ask.

"You mean your bulge?" Uume asks with a shrug. "Why not put it to some good use with a threesome?"

"It's not about Dex's bulge," Jamie says. "It's about me."

"It's about our relationship," I say, "which has been going downhill for some time."

"Time to revive it," Uume says. "Pretty boys that both of you are. I'll be the catalyst." He chucks his stylish gray flannel pants. White briefs come into view, filled with the largest bulge on the planet. I can't help it, I'm transfixed by this display. And little Jamie can't help it either. He's been crying, but his tears are evaporating, and a beautiful protuberance blossoms in his underwear.

"Okay," Jamie says. "I think I've seen the light. Dex, please forgive me. I'll explain later." He gets up, sheds his drawers, and reclines on the king-size bed, supine, aroused. He touches himself. "Take me, Uume," he says.

"No threesome?" Uume asks. "How about a blow job? Some fussy foreplay? We're in Florence, boys. Rimming was invented here. We owe it to the Renaissance."

"Take me," Jamie insists. "I'll explain later."

Uume looks at me. "Better he has sex with you than no sex at all," I say.

Uume shucks his snow-white briefs. There it undulates, his organ of uncountable inches, mounted on a ball sack of Kenyan glands and kissed by an afternoon sun, which, at this critical moment, has decided to filter through the window and turn his cock into a celebration of gleaming skin. His erection fills the room—nay, the entire solar system.

"No foreplay? You sure?" he asks Jamie. He peers at his organ, pushes it down with a flat hand, and watches it rebound. *Booiing.* He repeats the gesture as if to query his own virility. *Booiing.*

"I'll explain later," Jamie says. "Just take me."

Uume points at his inches. "No lube? You sure?"

"Spit," Jamie says as he tosses a rubber from the nightstand, where it has sat for days on end, unused. "Ask Dex to spit."

"A threesome after all," Uume says as he rolls the rubber on.

"Spit, both of you," Jamie says.

We spit, saliva soon dripping off the black manhood in all directions. Jamie clutches his dick, widens his legs, and offers the little caldera of his hole to our African friend.

"It'll hurt," Uume says.

"That's the idea," Jamie replies.

And there we go; Uume is in.

"*ARGH!*" Jamie yells. "*ARGH!*" And, before we know it, he comes. He comes with plentiful ropes of pent-up jizz, but still, he comes much too early.

"I've barely . . ." Uume stutters. "Sorry . . . I've barely . . . this has never happened to me before, and I've, you know . . ."

"Sorry," Jamie says. "Let me explain."

Another penny drops. I'm not particularly bright, but *Pellegrino*, it suddenly dawns on me, is also mineral water. Like Pellegrino, the mysterious art historian Jamie works with. Coincidence?

"You haven't been taking lessons in art history," I say to Jamie. "No," Jamie says with a frown. "I've been duped by this Pellegrino into . . ." The bedside phone suddenly rings. Nobody has used it in years, but now it rings. I pick it up. It's Luigi, asking me if he can speak to *leetle* Jamie.

"So, you knew that Jamie was in?" I ask.

"Something had to be done," Luigi replies. "Something had to be provoked. *È vero.* You only had to put two and two together." His good friend Giovanni is with him below and he's asking if they can come up and sort things out.

I gaze at Uume and his everlasting, sun-kissed erection. "We are not presentable at the moment," I say. "Our friend here has a priapic erection."

"Did it work?" Luigi asks.

"Did what work?"

"The erection."

I scan the expression of Jamie's angelic face. "Yes," I say.

"I thought so," Luigi replies, and promptly hangs up.

Will they be coming up or not, I wonder, while Jamie explains—more to Uume than to me—what you might've already guessed: Jamie despairing about the vortex in our relationship, scouring the Internet for solutions, and getting duped into this Florentine therapy by an under-endowed shrink. But the moment Uume chucked his pants ten minutes earlier—Jamie explains—he suddenly saw the light.

And there we are.

There's a knock on the door. Uume, standing in the middle of the room, looks at his sunlit boner. "No way to get rid of it without an ejaculation, boys. You want me to hide in the bathroom?"

"No—no," Jamie says. "I have an idea. Let them come in." Luigi has obviously been wielding his universal key-card, and a Roman nose pokes into the room a second later. Jamie, half-erect again, whispers something to Uume, who touches himself into full Kenyan arousal—stroking what by now has grown into the largest penis of the galaxy.

"Watch him," Jamie says to Giovanni.

"Watch him," Luigi says to Giovanni.

And there, at last, it works, the understated crotch of our wannabe billionaire shows unmistakable signs of life, far exceeding anything that was there before.

"Another case of a Renaissance willie?" Uume asks.

"Solved," Luigi says. He sidles up to the African, clutches the black dick the way Italian hotel managers clutch black dicks, and asks, "*Signore* Mkubwa, can I count on your further cooperation in this urgent matter?"

"Sure," Uume says. "We need to solidify results, after all." He grabs for Giovanni, pushes the man to his knees, and rams his galaxian prick down the faux-billionaire's throat. Meanwhile, Jamie has been spreading his legs for my cock. "I will always love you, Dex," he says.

And what of Luigi? Luigi has duly stripped, but doesn't know what to do. Uume has taken note. He lifts Giovanni up and hauls him across the room, releasing him onto the floor in front of the hotel manager. "Luigi," he says, "move into receptive position, and let's observe how a Roman nose can fuck your hotel manager's ass."

FORWARD INTO THE PAST

Richard Michaels

He was naked, he was gorgeous, and he had a gun aimed at me, and that complicated matters.

"Did I do something to upset you?" I asked. "Not everybody likes my sexual technique, but the complaints aren't usually so drastic."

"You don't remember me, do you?"

"Yes. You're the guy I just fucked."

"Again."

"I'm really flattered that it seems as if we made it more than once, but—"

"Do you recognize this?" he asked and turned around.

On the outward curve of his left buttock was tattooed a rose.

"I've deflowered you more than once?"

The flesh flora did seem familiar.

"Yeah," he said bitterly. "You've fucked me over before."

"Well, I'm sorry."

"And even now, you're ready to go again, aren't you?"

He pointed to my crotch, and I was a tad ashamed to see that he was right. My prick was absolutely erect and directed at my accuser like a beckoning finger. Since I was as nude as he was, there wasn't anything I could hide behind.

"That's one of my things," I said. "Well, obviously that's my *thing*, but what I mean is, excitement excites me, and you having a gun is stimulating in more ways than one. Plus, you're a good-looking guy, a nude good-looking guy I just enjoyably screwed, and so everything is combining in—*this*," I said, gesturing to my eager dick and waving it at him in the hopes that it would entice him to forget any harm he planned to inflict on me and return with me to the pleasures of the flesh—and his flesh had definitely been pleasurable.

"I'm Tom," he said.

"Are you sure?" I asked.

"What are you talking about?"

"Earlier, you told me that your name was Dan. In fact, I think that I may have yelled out 'Dan!' at a few auspicious times. Just as you yelled 'Jerry' more than once."

"Yeah, well, you're really good at screwing people."

"I think your *entendre* there is at least double. You seem to feel that I previously took advantage of you in several ways. And now that we've established that, perhaps you'll fill in the details."

"As you just filled me, in a different manner, of course. In any case, it wasn't even a year ago that I came to the great Jerry Jade to find my lover."

"He'd disappeared?"

"Not much gets past you."

"You really do dislike me, don't you? Which, under the, shall we say, *damp* circumstances, seems just a trifle odd. Didn't I find him?"

"Yeah, you found Mack. The great private eye was successful in his quest."

"That should have made you happy."

"It did, until I found out how you made each other happy."

"Ah, the pieces are beginning to fit."

"That was the problem. Your piece fit all too well into his piece."

"You know, Tom, Dan, whoever, I don't force people to have sex with me. Did I force you to have sex with me?"

"Oh, everybody knows that you're fucking irresistible and irresistible fucking."

"I have my charms, I've been told."

"Well, you'd think that you might occasionally keep a lock on those charms, especially when you're screwing the client's boyfriend."

"Perhaps," I said, "you should have all the parts of a story before you make a judgment."

"You're standing there naked with your stiff prick sticking out, turned on because I've got a gun on you, and nothing on me, and you're going to take some high moral attitude?"

"Yeah, that would seem a little incongruous, wouldn't it? Nevertheless, along with me pointing my dick at you pointing your gun at me, I want to point out a few other things."

He laughed—well, smirked, at least. "How could I resist hearing more of this witty, scintillating crap?"

Good. As long as he was amused, sort of, he wasn't shooting me.

"I remember you," I continued. "I recognized you when you approached me in the bar. And I certainly was familiar with that ass and that rose."

His sneer got back some of its rage, and I hurried on before he decided to use his gun as more than a prop.

"I was curious to see how far things would go. Well, I was curious to see how far you would go. So, we came back here, and I found out. I do know you and I remember your case."

From the moment he walked into the bar, I had felt such a *vu* that was decidedly *déjà* that I had to investigate. Wasn't that what I did? Wasn't that on my business card? I kept changing gears—reverse, drive, neutral—jerking from present to past, back and forth, and I was getting more than slightly dizzy.

"You hired me about a year and a half ago to find your lover. And I found him. The problem was—well, one of the problems was—he didn't want to see you. You asked what he'd said, and I told you: the relationship wasn't working, he was tired of you and your tendency to overdramatize things, he wanted to get away from you without some sort of operatic farewell—his words, not mine—so he packed up everything while you were at work and moved out. He left you a note explaining the situation, including the fact that he didn't want you to try to contact him. Everything accurate so far?"

"Yes," he said, and clenched his jaw.

"You wanted to know where he was. And even though I didn't really think it was a wise idea, I gave you an address and a phone number because you were my client. You were going to leave my office, but that's when everything got sticky—so to speak. You were halfway out the door when you stopped. You turned around and you were crying. Well, you were weeping, actually."

"What's the difference?"

"You very quickly went from moist and moderate to wet and loud. Actually, you did that in more ways than one, but so did I."

"In other words, you took advantage of me."

"Well, let's see how that interpretation fits. You were howling and spurting tears." I supposed that I was a little harsher than necessary, but his reinterpretation of events was beginning to annoy me. This combined with the mixture of apprehension and stimulation that was causing my slightly confused prick to inflate and subside, and I was definitely disconcerted. "And suddenly, there you were in my arms, burbling against my chest."

"So, did you pat me on the shoulder, murmur comforting things into my ear, dry my tears, and send me home?"

"Well, no."

"You sure the hell didn't."

I began to care less that he had a gun.

"Are you deliberately rewriting things or is your memory playing tricks on you?"

"What do you mean?"

"I mean that pretty soon you were kissing me, and then you were pressed up against me, and among the things pressed against me, and definitely up, was your cock. And when you began kneading my crotch, and evidently needing my crotch, it was pretty obvious what you wanted."

"Who wouldn't want you? You're the captivating Jerry Jade," he said scornfully, but his heart didn't seem in his derision, and both his lower lip and the gun were trembling slightly. "You could have said no."

"Yes," I admitted, "I could have, and all things considered, I wish I had. But what man doesn't want to think that he can make someone feel better and, yes, I confess it, make himself feel good at the same time? You're an attractive guy, Tom, and you appealed to my libido as well as my empathy."

"So you fucked me," he said harshly.

"I prefer to think that I consoled you."

"Of course that's what you prefer to think."

"Well, you seemed pretty damn consoled. Especially the second time."

He flinched.

"You cocksucker," he said.

"I think we've already established that I'm a cocksucker, and a damn good one. You certainly seemed appreciative."

"Yeah, the full-service private dick."

Then, abruptly, he plopped into a chair. The hand holding the gun dropped between his legs, but his finger was still on the trigger. And tears were dropping from his eyes, or maybe his nose was running.

"But why did you make it with Mack?" he whispered. "Even if I accept what you said about you and me, which I don't, I still don't understand why you made it with Mack."

"That was a mistake," I said. "I regret that."

"Regret you did it or regret you got caught?"

"I didn't think that I was betraying a client's trust. Maybe I just didn't want to think that I was betraying a client's trust."

Mack and Tom were an attractive couple. They *had been* an attractive couple, I told myself then. They were a couple no longer. I was going to relay that information to Tom. I didn't plan to share Mack's motives for the split. There was no reason Mack and I couldn't enjoy a tussle or two.

I told myself further, in the long internal conversation I was having, that it wasn't as if I'd gone to find Mack with the idea of investigating him in depth. And if Tom was perhaps given to theatrical excess, Mack was inclined toward the flirtatious. I realized that when he unzipped my fly.

So, instead of doing any soul searching, I searched Mack's body and he searched mine, and we were both happy with what we found.

Then I returned to Tom, and things got messy. I should have known that they would. Hadn't I read Raymond Chandler? Hadn't I read Ross Macdonald? Hadn't I read *How to Be a Private Detective*, which I bought from the bargain books table at Barnes & Noble?

So now, here I was, back with Tom, and things were past muddled and had moved into chaotic.

And I hadn't helped matters by ending up in bed with him

again. I'd had a good time, a very good time, but at this point in my career, didn't I understand the law of the universe that says you always pay for the good times? I liked to think that I was reasonably bright, but sometimes, I could be awfully stupid. When he approached me in the bar and pressed his crotch against my leg, my intelligence vanished, and my dick took over.

And as long as we were discussing the whys and wherefores—

"*You* approached *me* at the bar," I said. "You and your cock. If you do despise me, why did you even speak to me, let alone have sex with me?"

"I didn't intend to have sex with you. That sort of happened. After all," he added sardonically, "you do have your charms, and I was looking for you."

My eyebrows skidded into my hairline.

"It's true. I wanted you to find Mack again."

"I thought that you'd seen Mack."

"We ran into each other, and we had a long conversation, just a conversation, and he got very talkative. He told me that he was living in a different place than where you located him. But he didn't tell me where he's living now. And I want you to find him."

"Why?"

"So I can blow his fucking head off. So I can blow both of his fucking heads off."

It shouldn't have been a surprise that hot revenge lurked in the heart of someone with such an attractive face and a delectable body. Wasn't that a cliché of fiction? And hadn't Tom shown that his emotions were more than a bit rickety? Still, I was somewhat taken aback by the fury in his eyes.

"I think that's a bad idea."

"Why do you care?"

"For one thing, I like you, despite everything."

"Oh, good. That and six dollars will buy me a cup of Starbucks."

"And you have a very nice ass, and I don't want to see it in prison," I said with my tongue at least partially in cheek, imaging my tongue in his cheeks because the gun and his nudity and my nudity and my tumescence and the whole situation were beginning to get to me.

He might have been mind reading, or perhaps reading the sign language of my cock, when he asked, "Are you thinking about my ass in prison or my ass in your bed?"

"Both," I answered, wondering when common sense was going to return to the section of my brain that had lost all blood to my uncontrolled horniness.

The whole crazy trajectory of this episode took another tilt when he said, "I'm thinking of my ass in your bed, too."

Suddenly, he was where he'd been before—twice—nude body pressed up against my nude body, and my cock was hard, his cock was hard, and our arms were around each other, and my brain was saying *Have you abandoned your common sense altogether?* I managed to exercise enough prudence to note that the gun was on the floor, and then so were we. I produced a condom.

"Where the hell did you get that?" he demanded. "You're naked! Were you hiding the damned thing under your tongue?"

"A good private eye is always resourceful," I said.

Then I flipped him over and admired the rose on his ass and the ass under the rose, and then I was plumbing his deeper flower.

I was going to keep my tempo leisurely. After all, this was my second exploration of the divergences of his internal byways, and although I can usually snap back fairly rapidly, so to speak, from sexual congress, two ruts so quickly in a row might require a little extra time for rejuvenation. And why hurry this charming intrusion into his alluring extrusion? But his ass was so delightful, and my cock had been doing its up and down and up and down routine for quite a while and was now definitely raring to go. And after a few moments, he was lifting and lowering his backside in effusive cooperation and alternately clutching and releasing my passionate prick and steadily inflaming its rising temperature. Really, this guy had one of the most talented asses I'd ever fucked.

So my attempt at a temperate tempo was pretty quickly defeated, and soon I was plunging and withdrawing and then plunging faster and more deeply with no restraint, and then he was yelling and I was yelping, and oblivion settled over me.

When I woke up, my hard-on had subsided—finally—and Tom was gone, the gun was gone, and I was partway between the postsex euphoria and the anxiety of wondering when he and his weapons would appear again: the next few minutes, the next few years, or maybe sometime in the future when I thought that I had forgotten his lovely construction and his unpredictable temperament.

Wasn't that—I tried to tell myself philosophically, or as philosophically as I could, depleted as I was of body fluids and the capability of coherent reasoning—wasn't that the code of private dickdom? Not to get involved, just fuck 'em and leave 'em, or get left by 'em, and then constantly watch our backs as we waited for the next strike?

But none of my armaments, mental or physical, could be raised at the moment, and no matter how hard I tried to resist, I gave up and fell back into sleep.

ABOUT THE AUTHORS

MICHAEL AMPERSANT has just published his second book of gay erotic fiction, *This Is Heaven*. His first book, *Green Eyes*, was a finalist for the Lambda Literary Awards of 2015. He taught Artificial Intelligence in his previous life.

DALE CHASE has written male erotica for twenty years with stories published in numerous magazines, anthologies, and collections. Her third erotic novel, *The Great Man*, was published by Lethe Press in September 2017. Chase lives near San Francisco.

LANDON DIXON's work has appeared in *Men, Freshmen, [2], Mandate, Torso,* and *Honcho*, and in such noted anthologies as *Ultimate Gay Erotica 2005, 2007,* and *2008,* and *Best Gay Erotica 2009, 2014,* and *Volume 3,* and in the short-story collections *Hot Tales of Gay Lust 1, 2,* and *3*.

WAYNE GOODMAN has lived in the San Francisco Bay Area most of his life (with too many cats). When not writing queer-oriented historical fiction, he enjoys playing Gilded Age parlor music on the piano, with an emphasis on women, gay, and Black composers.

T. HITMAN is the nom-de-porn of a writer who once worked for the late, great *Men, Freshmen, Unzipped, Torso*, and other fine homo-celebratory newsstand publications.

NELSON HOUSE lives in the Great White North with his cat and the snow. His short stories have been published in magazines, anthologies, online, and in audio format.

RHIDIAN BRENIG JONES lives in Wales with his husband, Michael, and French bulldogs, Coco and Cosette. He leads an adult literacy program and writes before work, when the three best things in his life are still asleep.

CLARE LONDON took her pen name from the city where she lives, loves, and writes. Most of her work features gay romance and drama with a healthy serving of physical passion, as she enjoys both reading and writing about strong, sympathetic, and sexy characters.

KENZIE MATHEWS's erotica stories have appeared in *Lesbian Lust, Lesbian Cops, Rumpledsilksheets: Lesbian Fairy Tales, Best Lesbian Erotica: 2011, Lust in Time: Erotic Romance Throughout the Ages, The Big Book of Bizarro*, and *Of Devils and Deviants*. Her work was also included in *Best Gay Erotica 2015*.

RICHARD MAY's short fiction has been published in his collections *Inhuman Beings* and *Ginger Snaps*, his series *Gay All Year* on Amazon Kindle, in anthologies like *Never Too Late, Best Gay*

Erotica, and *Outer Voices Inner Lives,* and in literary journals, including *Bay Laurel, Chelsea Station,* and *Hyacinth Noir.*

RICHARD MICHAELS has published frequently in gay men's magazines. One of his stories appeared in the Cleis Press anthology *Special Forces,* and he was recently featured in *Not Just Another Pretty Face* from Beautiful Dreamers Press. Other erotic explorations have been included in previous Rob Rosen anthologies.

KYLE E. MILLER currently lives, writes, and wanders across Michigan's bountiful lakes and forests. His fiction has previously appeared in *Betwixt Magazine, See the Elephant,* and *Lackington's.* He has no particular attraction to sculpture and in fact finds most of it rather dull.

VINCENT MEIS has published four novels: *Eddie's Desert Rose, Tio Jorge, Down in Cuba,* and *Deluge.* Recent stories have been published in two collections: *WITH: New Gay Fiction* and *Best Gay Erotica 2015.* He lives in San Leandro, California, with his husband.

GREGORY L. NORRIS lives and writes at the outer limits of New Hampshire. Follow his literary adventures at gregorylnorris. blogspot.com.

Author and artist **JORDAN CASTILLO PRICE** combines sarcasm and sincerity, wit and weirdness. Jordan is best known for the *PsyCop* series, an unfolding tale of paranormal mystery and suspense starring Victor Bayne, a gay psychic medium plagued by ghostly visitations. She's also penned a modern spin on vampires in *Hemovore.*

MICHAEL ROBERTS is an old hand at erotica, so to speak. He published stories in leading gay magazines, as well as in collections from Alyson Books and STARbooks Press, and he has appeared on cruisingforsex.com—literarily, not literally. He has been featured in several previous Rob Rosen anthologies.

ABOUT THE EDITOR

ROB ROSEN (therobrosen.com) is the critically acclaimed and frequently best-selling author of the novels *Sparkle: The Queerest Book You'll Ever Love, Divas Las Vegas, Hot Lava, Southern Fried, Queerwolf, Vamp, Queens of the Apocalypse, Creature Comfort, Fate, Midlife Crisis, Fierce,* and *And God Belched.* His short stories have appeared in more than 200 anthologies. You can find twenty of them in his erotic romance anthology, *Good & Hot.* He is also the editor of *Lust in Time: Erotic Romance Through the Ages, Men of the Manor, Best Gay Erotica 2015,* and *Best Gay Erotica of the Year, Volumes 1, 2,* and *3.*